# 15

# MINUTES

## BOOK ONE

# D. K. MAMULA

For Carla and Brittany,
the fastest readers in West Virginia




For Barry M.
Thanks for the inspiration

He graduated from high school on a Friday afternoon. By the time the sun rose on Monday morning, he was packed and gone, leaving little more than a goodbye note for the parents who had devoted their lives to raising him.

"Dear Mom & Dad,

I'm sorry, but I have to go. I have plans for my life and there's just no way they can happen here. Please try not to worry, I'll be alright. I'll write once I get where I'm going.

I love you both very much.

Your son,
Gene"

He always said he would be on the first bus out of town as soon as graduation was over. It turned out to be a couple of days later, but he went, none the less. His destination? The biggest city he could find and as far away from rural America as possible. He had big dreams, and they had nothing to do with plowing fields or shoveling manure.

Felix Eugene Phillips Jr.—referred to as Eugene by his mother, Junior by his father and Gene by everyone else—was a tall, good-looking young man. He had dark hair and facial features that were attractive and inviting.

Growing up on his parent's farm, he spent many hours working with his father. The work was exhausting and endless and he hated it, even though his physique benefitted from it. The well-defined muscles he had developed over the years were as good as any he could have produced by lifting weights in a gym, and the bronze glow of his suntanned skin glistened with sweat as he worked the fields in the high afternoon sun.

The few hours not spent doing homework and chores were devoted to his one creative outlet—music. Gene was drawn to the guitar at an early age, the connection between the boy and the instrument apparent from the moment he grasped it in his young hands, and he devoured any information he could find on the subject. He taught himself all the chords and fingering techniques and learned to read music, practicing relentlessly. By the start of his teenage years, he had become an accomplished guitarist and could play just about any type of music, but rock was his favorite.

"Those stalls ain't gonna clean themselves, you know."

"I'll do it when I'm finished," Gene answered without looking up.

"You'll do it now."

"Dad, I need to practice!"

"You don't need to practice that much to play what you play. Now put that thing away and get out to the barn!"

"All you care about is your stupid farm!"

"This stupid farm puts food in your mouth and clothes on your back AND it paid for *this*!" Felix snatched the guitar from Gene's hand.

"Give that back!" Gene reached for the instrument and Felix jerked it away, banging it against the end table behind him. "You're gonna break it!!"

"Go out there and CLEAN THOSE STALLS!!"

"You don't give a damn about me! You never have!!"

"Eugene!" Ruby's sharp tone made the boy's head snap sideways to look in her direction.

Gene's chest rose and fell with quick breaths, his jaw clenched tight, his eyes moist with angry tears. He stalked out of the house and slammed the door causing several framed family photos to vibrate on the walls in his wake.

Ruby waited for the air to calm, then stepped closer to her husband and placed her small hand around the neck of the guitar; he relinquished it without argument. "Felix…"

"I don't wanna hear it, Ruby. As a member of this family, he has responsibilities. If he shirks those responsibilities, I'm gonna call him on it."

Ruby let the matter drop. She laid the guitar down gently in its case and closed the lid. Felix stood watching her for a few moments before his stern expression dissolved; he sighed.

"I know."

Ruby turned. "Excuse me?"

"I said, I know."

"What do you know?"

"I know Junior hates farm work. I know Junior doesn't want to be a farmer. I know how much he loves playing that guitar…" Ruby moved over to him and wrapped her arms around his middle. "…and I know my son hates me."

"No, he doesn't."

"Yes, he does, I can see it in his eyes every time he looks at me."

"He's a teenager, Felix, they're all a little rebellious at his age."

"It's more than that, Ruby. He despises everything about this life—the work we do, the way we live—everything we've worked all these years to build for him. He despises me more than any of it cause I'm the one keeping him here."

"Felix, that's not true..."

He kissed her on the forehead, pulled away and quickly went outside before she could finish. She watched her husband as he walked out toward the field, occasionally wiping the perspiration from his face. Ruby knew he was wiping away tears as well. She moved her eyes in the opposite direction and could see Gene working in the barn, angrily stabbing the pitchfork into the hay and tossing it out of the stalls, sending hay dust and straw swirling through the air around him. She adored them both and knew they each had great love for the other. She also knew they shared a stubborn streak, a trait passed down from father to son, and neither wanted to be the one to back down in a disagreement.

"Lord, give them peace..." she prayed aloud, "...and give me strength!" Ruby shook her head and laughed to herself as she headed to the kitchen to start dinner.

# CHASING THE DREAM

## Chapter 1

The security guard stepped over to the bench and tapped the sleeping man's shoulder. Gene looked up; the bright white glow of the fluorescent bulbs above him made his blurry eyes sting. The guard said nothing as he motioned with his thumb toward the exit. Gene gathered his belongings and left the bus station doing his best to maneuver through the mass of pedestrians that traveled the sidewalk at all hours. As he neared the curb, he bumped into a stocky, dark-haired man.

"Sorry."

"Asshole!" the man shot back without stopping.

Gene made his way across the thoroughfare and stepped into a coffee shop. He sat on a stool at the long counter.

"Coffee?" the server asked.

What he really wanted was a hot cup of coffee with some bacon and eggs, but he didn't have much to spend and needed to find a place to live before the day was out.

"Um… can I just have a glass of ice water, please?"

"Sure," she answered, feigning a smile. She stepped away from the counter and poured water from a pitcher into a small glass. She set it in front of Gene and held out a straw.

"Thanks."

"Mmhmm."

Gene unwrapped the straw and took a sip. A couple seats away, an older man was reading the morning paper. Gene borrowed the classified section and began sorting through the many listings for apartment rentals in the city. As he read, a man about the same age as himself with a medium build approached him from the far end of the lunch counter.

"How's it going?"

Gene looked to his right. "Good, thanks."

"You a musician?"

"Yeah." He inched his guitar case closer to him.

"Me, too, I'm Mike." The stranger stuck his hand out; Gene shook it.

"Gene."

"Looking for an apartment?" Gene didn't answer. "There's a couple open in my building. I could show you…"

"Thanks, but I'm good," Gene told him as he pointed to the classifieds.

"You're not gonna find anything in there that's in your budget."

"You don't know that."

"Ah, but I do."

Gene smiled at the man. "I appreciate the gesture, but I'll be fine."

"Okay, go ahead and look. Like I said, you're not gonna find anything in your budget."

"You don't know anything about my budget," Gene countered without moving his eyes from the newspaper.

Mike laughed. "Why'd you order water, Gene?" He looked at Mike but didn't respond. The server, who was cleaning the counter behind Mike, just smiled. "Listen, you need two things to survive in this city, a friend and a decent place to sleep. You just made a friend, and that friend can get you a decent place to sleep. It's kinda run-down, but it's definitely within your budget."

"Why would you help your competition?"

"You're no competition for me," Mike told him as he patted the guitar case, "I play the sax. Come on!" They picked up Gene's bags and started for the door. "Hang on a sec." He went back to the counter. "Hey Lucy, can we get a couple coffees to go, please?" Mike turned to Gene. "You take it black?"

Gene smiled. "Cream and sugar."

"One black and one with cream and sugar for my new friend, Gene."

Chapter 2

Gene stepped off the city bus onto the cracked concrete of the sidewalk. His eyes scanned the rows of stores that lined the downtown streets. Their windows sported many signs—'No Soliciting', 'No Loitering', 'Do Not Block Driveway', 'Keep Sidewalk Clear'—obviously put there to discourage aspiring artists such as himself from performing on the sidewalk outside their businesses. There were a lot of those little signs.

He was jerked from his thoughts by the rattling of the metal security gate that protected the storefront behind him. Once the gate was rolled up and locked in place, the proprietor flipped the sign on the door to 'OPEN'; he turned to Gene.

"Did I scare ya?"

"A little," Gene answered with a nervous smile.

The man laughed. "Sorry 'bout that."

"It's okay."

"I don't recall seeing you before, are you new in town?"

"I just moved here yesterday."

"Welcome to the big city!"

"Thanks." Gene's nervous smile returned.

He motioned toward the guitar case Gene was carrying. "I see you're a musician."

"Yeah... I'm sorry for blocking your store. I'll move..."

"You don't have to leave, I like musicians. I've been known to tickle the ivories now and then myself. You lookin' for a place to set up?"

Gene nodded. "Any suggestions?"

"Why not here?"

"In front of your place?"

"Yeah."

"You really wouldn't mind?"

"Not at all! A little music always makes the day better! You wait here, and I'll get you a stool." The man turned toward the door, then stopped and looked back at Gene. "You can play that thing, can't you?"

Gene laughed. "Yeah, I can play."

The man smiled and disappeared into the store. He returned a minute later with the stool as promised. "Here ya go," he said, "and here's some coffee for you." He held the cup out to Gene.

"Oh, thank you."

"You can plug your amp in over here…" The store owner began to unravel the power cord of the amp.

"I can do that. You don't have to…"

"It's okay, I know how it works. Besides, the outlet's a little hard to reach. Go ahead and drink your coffee while it's hot, I got this."

Gene took a few sips as he watched the man weave the cable around shelves and various pieces of merchandise. The rich flavor of the brew reminded him of his home and waking up to the smell of fresh coffee. He remembered lying in his bed, his mind still foggy with sleep, as the aroma of the coffee mingled with scents of sizzling bacon and spicy sausage as they fried in the cast-iron skillet alongside fresh eggs. Every so often, he would hear the familiar slapping sound the pancakes made as his mother flipped them on the griddle. What he wouldn't give for a breakfast like that right now.

"There you go, all set!" The man grinned at him.

"Thanks."

"How's the coffee? Hot enough?"

"It's good, thanks."

"Hey, I picked up some fresh crullers on my way in this morning. Hang on a sec, I'll grab one for you."

"No, wait…" He was through the door before Gene could finish and returned just as quickly with the pastry wrapped in a napkin.

"Here you go!" He offered it to Gene, who stood with cup in one hand and guitar case in the other.

"Um…"

"I'll just set it over here," he said as he placed the donut on a shelf close by.

"Thanks."

"You're welcome. Well, I better get to work. Good luck!" Gene nodded, and the man left him. A moment later the storekeeper poked his head out through the doorway. "By the way, the name's Eddie."

"I'm Gene."

"Have a great day, Gene!"

"You, too!"

The man ducked back into the deli and left Gene to his own devices. After a few more sips of coffee, he set the cup down beside the cruller, took the guitar from its case and connected the two ends of the guitar cord to their corresponding jacks on the amp and the instrument. He turned the amp on, then pulled the pick across the strings and adjusted the volume and tone.

Gene sat on the stool and lightly strummed the guitar as a few curious people stopped to listen. He mentally noted their presence, but kept his attention focused on the instrument without acknowledging them. The more he played, the more pedestrians he attracted, and it wasn't long before a clog of bodies had formed near the deli's entrance. Gene's heart began to palpitate as his trembling fingers tripped along the fretboard. He tried to pull himself together, but it was getting harder and harder to make his hands do what he wanted.

The optimistic expressions on the faces of the people who had gathered transformed to looks of disappointment. There were a few kind souls who dropped coins into his open case, more from pity that anything else, but the majority just turned and walked away.

He stopped and sat on the stool, his gaze focused on the sidewalk and away from the remaining eyes of the crowd. For the first time in all the years he had been playing, he was afraid. Playing in front of people had never been an issue in the small community of Bridgeville, where everyone knew everyone else, there were no strangers. Here, in this huge melting pot, everyone was a stranger. Not one of these people had any clue who he was, and he was sure a good portion of them didn't give a damn. He closed his eyes and tried to breath as deeply as he could.

"Gene?" A hand touched the young man's shoulder. "Hey, Gene." He looked up at Eddie; the man smiled. "A little nervous?"

Gene couldn't speak. The desert dryness that had overtaken his mouth and throat wouldn't allow him to form any words without choking on them.

"It's okay, happens to all of us." Eddie handed him a bottle of water; Gene took in several swallows. "You'll be fine in a minute."

"I don't think so, I feel like I might throw up."

"Just take a few deep breaths…"

"I don't think I can do this."

"Sure, you can!"

Gene shook his head. "No, I can't!" He slid off the stool and began unplugging the equipment.

"What are you doing?"

"I'm leaving, I'm going home!"

"You've only been here for half an hour, Gene!"

"I can't do this, Eddie!"

"So, you lied to me then."

"Lied to you? I didn't lie to you..."

"You told me you could play that thing!"

"I can play it."

"Yeah, well, talk is cheap."

"I can..."

"I don't believe you!"

"I said, *I CAN PLAY*!"

*"PROVE IT!"* They glared at each other for several seconds, both waiting for the other's next move. "That's what I thought." Eddie shook his head. "Why did you even come here? See ya 'round, Gene." He turned and headed back inside.

Gene stood alone in front of the deli. Whatever was left of the curious crowd had dissipated as folks got on with their lives. He looked around at the city streets, bustling with energy. There was no beginning or end, just a limitless supply of people on their way to or coming back from places unknown to the others. Bodies filled every inch from the subway tunnels that ran beneath the city streets to the tops of the massive skyscrapers that reached for the clouds. It was all one big continuous cycle.

He sat down on the stool and thought about Eddie's question. Why *did* he come here? There was only one reason—the music. It inspired him to create, spoke to him in ways no human had ever spoken before. It was the driving force behind his decision to leave home. That's way he came here, for the music.

Eddie made change and thanked his customer, then glanced through the window at Gene. The fledgling musician gazed at his guitar and caressed it as a man would a woman. He watched as Gene reattached the amp cable to the instrument, adjusted the knobs and plucked at the strings.

"C'mon, play something!" Eddie urged under his breath.

As if in response to Eddie's request, Gene rested the guitar on his lap and picked out a melody. He closed his eyes as instinct took over, his nimble fingers dancing across the strings faster and faster. The fear he felt was no match for the music that demanded to be heard.

Eddie watched as passers-by stopped to listen, drawn in by the astounding talent of the young performer. Many of the pedestrians bobbed their heads to the rhythm while others stared in wonder. They commented to each other about this stranger who plays the guitar.

A customer stepped up to the counter to pay for his merchandise. "That's some guitar player," he said.

"He sure is!" Eddie agreed with a bright smile. He rang up the order and thanked the man. When he looked out the window again, he noticed the crowd had grown, and even people inside the store were straining to see outside.

Eddie walked to the front door and leaned on the door frame; arms crossed. Gene played through, the music consuming all his senses. Afterward, he sat quietly on the stool, out of breath, sweat glistening on his brow.

A moment later, he heard it. Applause. He looked up at the crowd that had accumulated around him, all the faces that had been watching. He could hear the muffled thud of coins as they hit the padded inside of his guitar case. He smiled and thanked them for their generosity.

As the group began to thin, Gene saw Eddie standing in the doorway. The storekeeper smiled at him and went back inside.

"Hey, kid, can you play any Elvis?" an older gentleman asked.

"What song?"

"How about 'Love Me Tender'?"

Gene thought for a moment, then began to gently pluck the strings. The man took his wife in his arms and danced with her as Gene played. When the song was over, the man dropped a couple of dollar bills into the guitar case.

"That was nice," the man complimented, "thanks."

"You're welcome."

Gene sighed. The music, that was the answer. Just relax and let the music speak for itself.

## Chapter 3

September had arrived, and the change of seasons had begun earlier than expected. The deceiving brilliance of the afternoon sun fooled many of the city's occupants into being unprepared for the biting autumn chill that whipped around them. Though the streets were as busy as always, most folks made their trips short and sweet.

With the change in weather came a change in income for Gene. The citizens were gracious but didn't want to stand out in the cold for too long, and his audiences grew smaller and smaller. Still, he was there every day, playing his heart out in front of Eddie's place and doing the best he could to scrape by on whatever tips he made.

On days when the weather chased him indoors, he would work in the deli for Eddie, cleaning the storeroom and stocking shelves in return for a couple deli sandwiches and a little cash under the table. If he made enough in tips, he would offer to buy the sandwiches, but Eddie always refused to accept his money.

"You just keep playing out front," Eddie would say, "your guitar is good for business!"

He finished the song he was playing and thanked the few people who had stopped to listen. His numb fingers throbbed in unison with his head and the feeling in his toes was starting to wane. He had been playing since eight that morning and had intended to stay as long as he could because he needed the money, but a quick glance at the coins in his case assured him it wouldn't make too much of a difference one way or the other. With a heavy sigh, he packed up for the night.

Gene leaned against the door of the deli and maneuvered the guitar and amp through the opening. He walked up to the counter and set the amp on the floor in front of him, then set the case on top of it. Eddie, who was sorting the day's receipts, watched Gene as he looked over the selection of candy bars, finally choosing one and placing it on the counter.

As he began to count out the change in his hand, an older teen who was passing behind him suddenly reached for the guitar case, grasping just enough of the handle to be able to pull the case from where it sat. Without hesitation, Gene's hand clasped the remaining part of the handle, sending the various coins showering to the floor around them. The two held tight to the case, yanking it back and forth in a desperate tug-of-war.

Eddie calmly reached under the counter, retrieved the Louisville Slugger that he kept on hand for such occasions and rested it against his shoulder. When the teenager caught sight of the baseball bat, he stopped pulling and quickly glanced from the bat to the case and back again, as if calculating the odds of getting away with the instrument versus getting pummeled by Louisville's best. Eddie glared at the boy and tightened his grip around the handle of the bat. Finally, the teen let go of the case and took a few cautious steps backwards before turning and bolting through the door.

Gene checked the case over, making sure there was no damage, then laid it on the floor and opened it. He took the instrument out and ran his fingertips along its smooth edges, checking for any chips or scratches that might have occurred during the struggle.

"Everything good?"

"I think so." Eddie walked around the counter and stooped down to pick up the scattered coins. He handed them to Gene, who looked at them and laughed. "You know, you really didn't have to bother with the change."

"You worked all day for that."

"Yeah," Gene scoffed as Eddie walked to the opposite side of the counter and returned the bat to the shelf underneath. "Hey, thanks…"

"You're welcome."

"Don't know what I'd do if I lost my guitar." They shared a smile. "Um, how much do I owe you?"

"Don't worry about it."

"No, really, how much?"

"It's on the house, I'll just put this in a bag for you…"

"I don't need a bag for a candy bar, Eddie…

The merchant pulled a plastic grocery bag from the rack and loaded it with two deli sandwiches, a couple bottles of soda and the candy bar. He tied the handles of the bag closed and handed it to Gene.

"There you go!" he said with a smile.

"Eddie, I don't have enough to pay for all that…"

"I told you, it's on the house."

"But…

"Gene, you've had a bad day, let me do something to make it better."

The young man sighed. "Thanks." He took the bag from Eddie and picked up the guitar case and amplifier.

"See you tomorrow?" Eddie asked.

Gene smiled. "Yeah. Goodnight."

"Goodnight."

## Chapter 4

The bus stopped, and Gene exited, guitar in one hand, amp and deli bag in the other. As the vehicle pulled away, he stood facing the haunting edifice on the opposite corner.

The building was dilapidated and dirty with crumbling red bricks and rain gutters that were only partially attached to the rotting wooden eaves. Several of the windows were cracked or broken, while others were completely missing, their openings having been boarded up long ago. Any intact glass that remained had been caked in grit and grime by years of city smog.

The black wrought iron fire escape that weaved its way down the outside of the building was of little use since the metal had eroded beyond repair. It wasn't the safest place to live, but in a neighborhood like this—with all its unsavory characters, as his mother would say—it was much safer than sleeping on the streets, and if he was late with a rent payment now and then, the landlord didn't hound him about it. They were happy to rent the place for whatever they could get for it. The fact that the city bus stopped close by didn't hurt either. The less time he spent traveling back and forth, the more time he could spend playing and earning money. Besides, it was all he could afford for the tips he was making.

Gene walked up to the door of the aging apartment building and entered the spacious foyer. His feet felt heavy as he trudged up what tonight seemed like 500 steps to the third floor. As he passed the various doors, he could hear the other tenants going about their lives—the middle-aged couple in 1B was arguing again; Theresa, the young, single mother in 2D, was singing her baby to sleep; 3A's TV was blaring away—all of them oblivious to his comings and goings.

He put his key into the lock of apartment 3F, opened the door and stepped through, then quickly closed the door and fastened the deadbolt. He dropped his keys on the small kitchen table, along with the bag from the deli, and rested his guitar case and amp on the floor by the door.

Gene sat down at the table and glanced around at the contents of the small, lonely room. There wasn't much to see—an old armchair with fabric worn so thin you could see the stuffing under it; a loveseat with broken-down springs that doubled as his bed; an end table and lamp that he was sure had been around since the 1960's and a wobbly two-seater dining table and chairs. There was a small Frigidaire that worked well enough, but no stove. He had to use a hotplate he borrowed from the nice lady in 1C; she had an extra one. This was home—at least for now—and he was grateful to have it, but he couldn't help feeling there was more than this in store for him. His eyes settled on the curved black case. His guitar was his saving grace; his music was the one thing he was sure about. Earlier at the deli, he had almost lost it all.

Gene's stomach rumbled against his ribcage and he rubbed his midsection. He removed the food from the bag, unwrapped it and took a huge mouthful, chewing three or four times before the next bite, and then again before the next. Without realizing it, he had devoured the entire sandwich. He sat back in the chair and closed his eyes as he swallowed the last few morsels. A few satisfied moments passed, until the calm was broken by his growling stomach demanding more sustenance. Gene eyed the second sandwich. He had decided on the way home that he would eat one for dinner and save the other for tomorrow's breakfast. It was a good idea, he thought, the smart thing to do… but he was *so hungry*. He stared at the food, trying to resist the urge to open it. As he battled his hunger pangs, Gene looked over at the Snickers bar that Eddie had included in this generous little grab-bag. He decided that he could eat the candy bar for breakfast, and this one night, he would go to bed with a full stomach. With a smile and a light laugh at the thought of how his mother would definitely *not* approve of his meal choices, he peeled back the cellophane from the second deli sandwich.

## Chapter 5

Eddie stood the broom in the corner behind the counter. He retrieved two sodas and a couple of sandwiches from the cooler and took them over to a small table against the far wall, then motioned for Gene to join him.

"That's enough work for tonight," he said as Gene sat across from him, "let's BS for a while."

Gene popped the lid off the soda bottle and took a drink, then set it down on the table and began unwrapping his sandwich. Eddie watched him for a minute without speaking.

"So, how are things going?" Gene shrugged as he chewed a small bite of his sandwich. "Gene?" The young man looked up. "You all right?"

"Yeah."

"You sure?"

"Yeah, why?"

"Just wondered. You seem a little down-in-the-mouth lately." Eddie took a bite of his food. "Thought you might need someone to talk to."

Gene hesitated. "It's nothin' really," he answered, trying to blow it off. He took another sip of soda and poked at the sandwich. "I've just been thinkin' about my family."

"Feelin' homesick?"

"A little," Gene admitted, "I really miss my mom and dad."

"Is this the longest you've ever been away from home?"

"Yeah." He broke a small piece off the sandwich and nibbled at it.

"We all feel that way from time to time, it'll pass." Eddie took another bite. "I'm gonna grab a bag of chips, you want some?" Gene didn't answer. Eddie came back to the table with two bags. He tossed one to Gene, then pulled his own bag open as he sat down. "So, are you going to tell me what's really on your mind?"

"What do you mean?"

"I know homesick when I see it, Gene, this is more than that, now spit it out."

Gene fidgeted in his chair. "I think it's time for me to go back."

"Home?" Gene nodded. "You mean for a visit, right?"

"For good."

"Why?"

"Eddie, I've been here for almost two years. I keep writing and playing and singing and working and nothing is happening. Other than a few decent tips and a few nice compliments, nobody gives a damn."

"But somebody will..."

"I don't think so."

"You can't leave now. If you do, you'll be wondering 'what if' for the rest of your life!"

"What if I stay and three years from now nothing's changed?"

"My business has *tripled* ever since you started playing out front. People I've never seen before, come in here and tell me they heard about this *unbelievable* guitar player and they had to come and hear it for themselves. The more customers that come in, the more money we *both* make, and the more people will hear you play! One day the right person will hear you and..."

"One day? Which day? Today? Tomorrow? Next Fourth of July??"

"Nobody can answer that, Gene, life is a game of chance. All I know for sure is if you don't take the chance, you can't win the game."

The two men looked at each other for a few moments, before Gene wrapped the remainder of his sandwich in its cellophane, swallowed what was left of the soda and stood from the table.

"Well, all I know is the 'right' person should have heard me play by now." He walked over to the cooler and slid the empty bottle into a slot in the box on the floor.

"I've seen 'em come and I've seen 'em go," Eddie said from his seat, "Some were good—some were *really* good—and a lot of them should never left home in the first place, but most of them didn't stay half as long as you have."

"That's what I'm saying, Eddie, I've been here *too* long! I'm just spinning my wheels!" He leaned against the counter and crossed his arms over his chest. "I must've been a fool to think I had the talent to make it in this business..."

"You *do* have the talent, Gene."

"Then why am I still singing on the sidewalk for spare change?"

"Give it some time..."

"I *have* given it time!"

*"Give it more!"* Eddie sighed, then stood and moved to face him. "Listen, I've been here for a while and I can honestly say you are the most talented musician that's come down the pike in quite some time, and you know that, or you wouldn't still be here. Now, I'm gonna give you my advice whether you want it or not."

Gene laughed. "Okay, go ahead."

"Don't quit. No matter how long it takes, don't give up. Don't quit. It's gonna happen for you, Gene, I can feel it. *It's going to happen for you!* Keep writing, keep playing, keep singing and just… *be patient*, okay?"

Gene smiled and nodded in agreement. "Okay." They gathered their belongings, shut off the lights and called it a night.

Chapter 6

The businessman moved smoothly along the congested sidewalk, following the flowing stream of pedestrians. When he reached the corner, he stopped briefly to check for traffic. He was in a hurry but getting flattened by a taxicab wasn't in today's plans, so he stood impatiently waiting as they zoomed past.

Amidst the rumble of automotive noise and the constant chatter of passers-by, he noticed the melodic sound of guitar music floating up from behind. A glance over his right shoulder revealed a young man standing in front of a local delicatessen, wielding an electric guitar; a small portable amp sat on the sidewalk beside him.

His interest peaked, he moved a few steps closer to the musician and stood listening to him play. When the music ended, the onlookers complimented him and dropped tips of various amounts into his open guitar case.

"Thanks folks," the player said. He unplugged his guitar from the amp and stooped down to retrieve the money they had left.

"Hey kid."

Gene looked up to see a well-dressed man in his early thirties. "Yeah?"

The man held out a five-dollar bill. "You're good."

"I know," Gene responded as he added the bill to his total earnings for the night.

The man laughed. "Do you now?"

"Yeah, I do."

"So, what's your name?"

The young man closed the guitar case and stood up straight. "Gene Phillips."

"Where you from, Gene?"

"What's it to you?"

"In the grand scheme of things, not a whole hell of a lot," the man answered. The boy had attitude, he liked that.

"Well, I'm from right here, right now."

"Okay, Gene Phillips from right here, right now, my name's Miles."

"First name or last?" Gene asked.

"What's it to you?" Miles countered; he handed Gene a business card. "See the number on that card, Gene? Give me a call at that number tomorrow. I've got something I'd like to discuss with you."

"What kind of 'something'?"

"Let's just call it a, um… an opportunity." Miles grinned at him. "You have a good night now, Gene."

Gene watched as the stranger walked away and was absorbed into the tangled mob of pedestrians that moved in every direction. He looked at the card once more before shoving it into the back pocket of his jeans, then gathered his equipment and headed back to his apartment on the south side.

## Chapter 7

"Gene!" Miles waved him over to a booth by the window; they shook hands. "Have a seat." The young man carefully set his instrument on the seat beside him and put the small amp under the table between his feet. "I see you brought your guitar."

"It goes where I go."

"You look hungry, let me buy you lunch…"

"I don't have a lot of time for chit chat, so why don't you just get to the point."

Miles sat back in the booth. "Okay, I will. I want to sign you."

"Sign me?"

"Sign you, represent you, manage your career," the man clarified with a smile, "I want to make you a star." Gene shook his head and laughed as he stood from the booth and picked up his guitar. "Wait, where are you going?"

"Listen… um, what's your name again? Miles? Every other person who walks by me on the street and likes the way I play tells me they can make me a star. I don't need someone to make me a star, I can do that myself. What I need is someone who can open a few doors for me…"

"I can do that."

"Yeah? Well, how about money? You got money, 'cause I don't, and every minute I stand here bullshittin' with you gets me deeper in the hole." The young man headed toward the door of the diner.

"How much do you need?"

"A million should do it!" he answered without stopping.

"Done!"

Gene turned and smiled. "You're funny."

"Why don't we make it two?"

"Nah, I don't want to take all your money," Gene joked.

"I'm not giving you all of it, just two million," Miles corrected him in a flat tone.

"You have two million dollars in the bank?"

"Yeah."

"And you're gonna give it to me?"

"Yeah."

"Why would you do that?"

"Think of it as an advance."

"An advance on *what*?"

"Anticipated royalties of future album sales."

"You're serious…"

"*Dead* serious," Miles said, "we can go to the bank and set up the account right now, if you'd like."

Gene glanced out the window at the afternoon sun. "It's gettin' late. I gotta go to work…"

"Okay, it's your call. If you prefer to drag that guitar and amp all over town, playing on street corners and hoping you'll make enough in tips to feed yourself for the next 24 hours, I won't stand in your way." He smiled as he patted Gene's shoulder and left the diner, walking over to a waiting limo; Gene followed.

"Hey," Gene called; the man turned. "*Who are you?*"

"I told you, my name's Miles, and this is just the first of many doors I can open for you," he said, gesturing toward the open door of the car, "The question is, are you willing to take a chance and step through it?"

Gene stared hard at Miles, then surveyed the streets around them. He watched as wannabes just like him hurried along the sidewalks, bobbing and weaving through the 'common' people, all of them determined to prove they've got what it takes to make it big. They seemed unaware of each other as they traveled through the overpopulated streets, their only objective being to get to that next gig, that next 'big break'. Everything around him flowed in a steady stream day in and day out, like blood pulsating through the city's veins. Gene looked back at Miles and the man gestured toward the open door again, but Gene didn't move.

"Like I said before, it's your call," Miles told him, "but let me ask you one question, Gene Phillips from right here, right now—" Miles leaned back against the car, crossed him arms and looked Gene straight in the eye. "—whatta ya got to lose?"

Images of long days spent playing his heart out for a few dollars' worth of coins only to return to a grimy little apartment and a dinner of cheap hotdogs boiled in a dented saucepan on a borrowed hot plate cycled through the young man's mind.

"Well?" Miles prodded.

Gene moved slowly toward Miles, pausing one last time before climbing into the spacious backseat of the limousine with his precious guitar and amp in tow. Miles waited, giving Gene time to settle into the comfortable interior of the automobile, to get a sense of what it feels like to be on the inside looking out instead of the other way around.

Miles smiled to himself. It was so easy to get them to bite—maybe too easy. All he had to do was dangle the proverbial carrot and the little rabbit would come running. He turned and slid into the seat as the chauffer closed the door.

Chapter 8

The limo pulled up to the curb in front of a towering structure in the uptown region of the city's business district. The chauffer opened the door and the car's occupants stepped out. Gene looked up at the sign on the front of the building—'National Bank & Trust'.

"Come on," Miles said as he and Gene entered through the large glass doors. Once inside, Miles walked up to one of the teller windows where a young woman promptly greeted him.

"Good afternoon, Mr. Sharpe, what can I help you with today?"

"Good afternoon, I wanted to speak to someone about opening a new account for my friend here…"

"I'd be happy to help you open that account, Mr. Sharpe," the bank manager offered, "If you'll step into my office, we can take care of the paperwork."

"Thank you."

The man led them to a posh corner office where they sat and filled out the necessary forms.

"And what amount will you be depositing in your new account today, sir?" the bank manager asked Gene.

"Um… I…"

"I'd like you to transfer two million from my business account into this one," Miles volunteered.

"Not a problem, Mr. Sharpe." The man tapped away at his computer keyboard, then retrieved some papers from the printer. "All right, Mr. Sharpe, I need you to sign and date these for me, please, to show that you have authorized the transfer of funds." Miles did as the man asked and handed the forms back to him. "Thank you, sir, and Mister…" He paused and looked at the papers to remind himself of Gene's name. "Mr. Phillips," the man said with a smile, "if you'll just sign here, I'll have a debit card printed for you."

Gene looked the forms over but hesitated to sign them.

"Miles, can I talk to you privately for a minute?"

"Of course, will you excuse us?" The bank manager nodded, and they stepped out into the lobby. "What's wrong, Gene?"

"You're giving me two million dollars."

"Yes."

"*Two million dollars... of your own money...*"

"I told you I would."

"I can't let you do that, Miles."

"Why?" Gene opened his mouth, but no words would come. "Gene, you can use the money, right?"

"Yes, I can use it, but..."

"But what?"

"Well, what if you need it for something?"

"Come here," Miles instructed as he returned to the teller window. "Young lady, would you please tell me the balance of my business account?" The bank teller promptly pulled up the information on her computer and jotted down the number, then passed the paper to Miles.

"There you are, Mr. Sharpe, will there be anything else?"

Miles glanced at the paper, then smiled at the teller. "No, thank you." He guided Gene away from the other bank customers before showing him the account balance; Gene's jaw dropped as he read the number. Miles leaned in toward him. "I think I can spare the money. Shall we?" Miles asked as he gestured toward the manager's office; Gene shook his head.

"I'm sorry, I know it sounds crazy, but I just can't take this money from you, Miles."

"*What is the problem, Gene?*"

"I haven't *earned* it."

Miles smiled as he led Gene back to the corner office where the bank manager was waiting.

## Chapter 9

Gene sat alone in his dreary one-room apartment staring at the bank card. He turned it over and over, the gold letters glistening in the light that shone through the window from the streetlights on the alley corner. He took a drink from his bottle of beer and was pondering the events of the day when a knock on his door broke the silence. Gene didn't react and the knock repeated.

"Gene, you home?" asked a muffled voice from the hallway. "Gene!" the voice called again, "Gene, it's me, Mike!" Mike tried the knob and the door opened, letting the light from the hallway cast a glowing triangle across the dingy hardwood floor of the dark apartment. As he stepped through, he saw Gene sitting in a chair near the window. He watched as his friend's silhouette took another drink from the beer bottle. "Got any more of those?"

"In the fridge," the figure answered without turning.

"Mind if I..."

"Help yourself."

"Thanks." Mike stepped over to the refrigerator and pulled a cold bottle from the carton. He twisted the lid off and took a swallow. "So, did you make any money today?"

Gene paused before answering. "Yeah, some."

"Really? Maybe I should start following you around. I barely made more than the bus ride home. Must have been Tight-Ass Day on that side of town." Mike laughed; Gene stayed silent. Mike took another drink from his bottle and sat down next to Gene. "So, what's the grand total?"

"You wouldn't believe me if I told you."

"Well, I know it was enough to buy beer."

"Yep," Gene confirmed, his eyes still fixed on the card in his hand; Mike watched him.

"Hey, you okay?"

"Yep."

"What's going on, Gene? Are you in some kind of trouble?"

Gene laughed. "No, I'm not in any trouble. In fact, I've had a very good day." He tipped the bottle back and drained the last of the beer, then stood and walked to the fridge to get another bottle, passing the card to Mike on the way.

"What's this?" Mike reached over and switched on the lamp. "It looks like a debit card."

"That's exactly what it is."

"You swiped somebody's debit card?"

"Nope, it's mine."

"But this is from National Bank & Trust."

"Yep."

"That's *uptown*, man."

"Yep."

"You have an account there?"

"Yep."

"Uptown… at National Bank & Trust? Where all those bigwigs keep their money?"

"Yep."

The two men stared at each other for several seconds. A grin formed across Mike's face.

"You know, you almost had me!" He laughed and shook his head. "It's that damn poker face of yours. Remind me never to play cards with you!"

"It's my account, Mike."

"Okay, fine, you have an account at a ritzy bank uptown. Whatever you say, Gene. Just make sure you give this card back to the bank in the morning. Doesn't matter how much money the poor sap has, it's not worth going to prison for…"

Mike laid the card on the end table next to the lamp. Gene walked over, picked up the card and handed it back to him.

"*Look* at it." He waited while his friend examined the front of the object again.

"Gene…"

"Yeah?"

Mike paused. "Gene, this card has your name on it." Gene nodded and took another drink. "Why does it have your name on it?"

"I told you, Mike, it's mine."

"This is *your* card?"

"Yes, it's my name, it's my card, it's my account."

"Is there any money in it?" Mike asked, half joking.

"Yeah."

"How much… that is, if you don't mind me asking?"

"A lot."

"How much is 'a lot'?" There was no answer. "Gene?"

"Two million."

*"Two million?"* Gene nodded. *"Dollars???"* Once again, Gene nodded. "Now I *know* you're messin' with me!" Gene looked

at his friend. "This card is connected to a bank account with a two-million-dollar balance? Under *your* name??"

"Yeah."

"So, you're a *millionaire*??"

"Apparently."

"Where in the hell did you get two million dollars?"

"I had a meeting with this guy named Miles. He said he wants to sign me and manage my music career."

"And?"

"And he set up the account and gave me the money."

"Some guy who likes your music gave you two million dollars?"

"Yeah."

"He just *gave* you two million dollars?"

"Yeah." Mike laughed out loud. "I know it sounds unbelievable, but it's true!"

"Did you sign with him?"

"Not yet."

"Good!"

"We're meeting again tomorrow morning at his office."

"You're not actually thinking about going, are you?"

"He seems legit, Mike…"

"Gene, it's a scam! You sign a contract and they give you an expense account, except it's *not real*. By the time you figure out what's happened, they're long gone with the rights to your music and you're left holding a phony bank card that's connected to an account that doesn't exist!"

"It's not a phony card."

"Gene…"

"I went to the bank with him, Mike! I was there when they set up the account!" He handed the bank forms to his friend. "Everyone in the bank knew him by name, they were practically tripping over each other to make him happy. The bank manager *himself* printed the debit card for me!"

"Holy shit…" Mike said as he sifted through the various pages of paperwork. "Have you tried to use the card yet?"

"That's how I got the beer," Gene answered; he switched off the lamp. The two aspiring musicians sat together in the darken room without speaking and finished their beers by the hazy glow of the alley streetlight.

Chapter 10

Gene arrived at the office building in the heart of the city and entered the spacious lobby. The security guard directed him to the elevators that would deliver him to the 17th floor where the offices of Sharpe Management could be found. The receptionist greeted him and notified her boss that his 'nine-o'clock' had arrived.

"Good morning, Gene."

"Good morning, Mr. Sharpe."

"Such manners! That's the sign of a good up-bringing." He smiled and shook Gene's hand. "I appreciate the politeness, but you can call me Miles from now on, okay?" Gene agreed. "Let's go talk in my office. Hold my calls, Diane."

Once inside, Miles closed the door. "Gene, I want you to meet my associates. Each of them oversees a different division within the company—production, wardrobe, publicity, sales and marketing, art and photography, research and development, A&R. I invited them here this morning so they could hear your music."

"Oh..."

"I like to get several opinions when I consider signing new talent. Are you comfortable with that?"

"Oh yeah, sure, it's fine with me..." He paused. "Good thing I brought my guitar!" Gene smiled as the others laughed. Miles retrieved a stool from the side of the room.

"You can have a seat right here, Gene."

The young man set the amp down and found an outlet on a wall a few feet away. He plugged the connecting cable into the jack on his guitar, then sat down on the stool and began plucking the strings one by one, turning the individual tuning keys to perfect the sound. Finally, he strummed all the strings together a couple of times, popped off the stool to increase the volume on the amp and then returned to his seat and strummed the strings again.

"Ready?" Miles asked. Gene glanced up at the group, smiled and nodded.

"Why don't you start by telling us a little about yourself?" Associate1 suggested.

"Like what?"

"Where are you from?"

"Not here."

Associate1 laughed. "Is that in the U.S.?"

"Yeah, somewhere in there."

Associate2 looked at him at him curiously. "How old are you, Gene?"

"Twenty."

"You've got a great body—" Associate3 commented.

"Yes, he does," Associate2 agreed.

"—do you work out a lot?"

"I used to."

"What about your parents?" asked Associate4.

"What about them?"

"What's their take on all this? I mean, you're only 20, you're still kind of young. Do they support your music or would they rather you go to college, get a degree?"

"They're not in the picture."

"So, where'd you learn to play?" Associate5 asked.

"At home."

"Yes, but who taught you, who was your instructor?"

"I didn't have one, I taught myself."

"You're self-taught?" Gene confirmed the man's statement. "You play by ear then?"

"Yeah… well, I did at first, until I learned to read music."

Associate4 sat up straighter in his chair. "Then you have had some formal music training?" he asked.

"No sir."

"You're *completely* self-taught?"

"Yes sir."

The associates began to harbor doubt about the young artist. They had auditioned self-taught musicians before, and those auditions almost always ended up with a 'sorry' or 'no thank you' from the company and a good bit of tears and resentment from the performers. The group fell silent as Gene waited.

"Gene, would you mind stepping out for a minute?" Associate4 requested.

"Sure." Gene pulled the amp cable from the jack on his guitar and went out to the lobby.

"Miles…" Associate1 began.

"I know what you're gonna say, but I'm telling you this kid is *different*."

Associate5 laughed a little and started to gather his papers. "Of course, he is."

"He's a smartass, too," Associate1 commented.

Associate4 agreed. "Yes, he definitely has an attitude."

"But we can use that," Associate2 said, "and with that body…"

"We can *absolutely* do something with that body!" Associate3 chimed in. The two women smiled at each other.

"Yeah, but a self-taught artist usually comes complete with a chip on his shoulder," Associate1 told them, "They can be a real pain in the ass to work with…"

"All I'm asking you people to do is *listen*!" Miles invited Gene back into the room. "My associates are interested in hearing you play."

"Okay." Gene plugged the amp cord into his guitar and resumed his place on the stool. "Um… what would you like to hear?"

"What do you like to play?" Associate3 asked.

"Well, I usually play rock, but I can play whatever…"

"How about that one you were playing that first night?" Miles interrupted. Gene thought for a moment, then began to play as the group quietly observed.

The budding musician played the piece as if it was flowing straight from his fingertips. Every note was smooth and clean, every chord progression flawless. He played riffs and runs in alternating tempos, using intricate fingering techniques as his hand traveled the entire length of the fretboard. When he finished, they applauded his efforts.

"Did you write that?" Associate1 asked.

"Yes sir."

"Very impressive."

"Yes, very," Associate4 agreed.

"Thanks."

"Do you sing?" Associate1 asked.

"A little."

"Would you sing something for us?"

Gene strummed the guitar, sending a gentle melody through the room. The group sat listening as he sang the lyrics to one of his favorite songs. Miles stood on the opposite side of the room watching their reactions. As the song ended, applause filled the room; Miles came around to meet Gene.

"Gene, would you mind stepping out again," Miles asked, "just for a couple minutes?" The group waited until the door closed behind the young man.

Associate5's eyes widened. "Where in the hell did you find him??"

"Playing on the sidewalk in front of a deli."

"And no one noticed him before *now?!*" Associate4 asked, astonished.

"Good ear, Miles," Associate1 complimented.

"Now we have to figure out what we're going to do with him!" Associate3 stated.

"What's his name again?" asked Associate5.

"Gene Phillips."

Associate2 scrunched up her nose as if she smelled something foul. "Gene Phillips?" They all sat silent. "Well, that won't work."

"Just leave that to me," Miles instructed, "What I need all of you to do is what you do best. I want a full workup on this kid— publicity, wardrobe, marketing—everything! I want him in the studio, and I want a single recorded and released within the next two weeks..."

"*Two weeks??*" Associate1 questioned.

"Two weeks! I want him on posters, billboards, the cover of every teen magazine on the market. I don't want to turn a corner, look at a TV screen or turn on a radio without seeing this kid's face or hearing his music. I want him *everywhere, all the time!* We need to create an image for this kid that *no one* will be able to ignore— now, make it happen!" As the associates gathered their notes and quickly headed out of the room, one of them stepped over to speak privately to Miles.

"So, how much of an incentive did you give this kid?"

"Two mill," Miles answered.

"That's a lot to risk on an unknown."

"I have every intention of doubling my investment."

The man smiled. "Feeling lucky, are we?"

Miles grinned at him. "You don't need luck when you've got a sure thing!" They laughed together as they exited the meeting room and the man went on his way. Miles looked over at Gene, smiled and motioned to him. "Why don't you come back into my office, Mr. Phillips, we have a lot to talk about."

## Chapter 11

Miles and Gene sat opposite each other; contract papers laid across the desk between them. Both men passed the forms back and forth, signing on the appropriate lines and initialing sections as necessary.

"Are you sure you don't want to have a lawyer check these over for you? I'd be happy not to enforce the contract or even void it completely…"

"No, that won't be necessary. It seems fair to me."

"Maybe we should wait until you can speak to someone, someone independent of the company that can explain all the legal jargon to you… someone who could look out for your best interests. You can afford a to hire a lawyer now, you have money in the bank."

"It's okay, Miles, really. I've read through it—well, some of it—and I haven't seen anything questionable. Basically, it says I make music and you pay me for it, right?"

Miles smiled at him. "Basically, give or take a few minor details." Gene signed the last form and handed it back to Miles, who placed his signature on the line below Gene's. Miles laid the pen down on the desk and walked around to shake Gene's hand.

"Welcome to the fold!"

"Thanks."

"Now that all the legal stuff is done, we can move on to the next step."

"The next step?"

"We need to find you a name."

"I have a name."

"We need to find you a *better* name."

"What's wrong with Gene Phillips?"

Miles sat back against the edge of the desk. "No offense, but 'Gene Phillips' could *never* be a rock star."

"Why not?"

"Because he's *'Gene Phillips'*," Miles explained with a light laugh, "You need a name that's edgy, but easy to remember, one that will send chills down the spine of every female who hears it. Now, I've given this a lot of thought and I believe I have found exactly what we're looking for…" He wrote down a name and passed it to Gene.

*"Xavier Kaine?"*

"It's perfect, right?"

"You really think 'Xavier' is easier to remember than 'Gene'?"

"Well, they're both easy to remember, but only one of them is easy to forget. No one will remember Gene Phillips, but Xavier Kaine…" Miles paused and smiled. "Xavier Kaine they will *definitely* remember!"

Gene looked doubtful. "I'm not sure about this, I mean, I was named after my father…"

"I thought you said your parents weren't in the picture."

Memories of his father filtered through Gene's mind. Some were good, but most were of the arguments they had about working on the farm and about Gene's music. He remembered how they never saw eye-to-eye on anything, how his father never believed in him, never said he was proud of his only child.

Gene looked back at the name on the paper. "I don't really feel like an 'Xavier'," he stated, still staring at the name in front of him.

"Just give it some time, Xavier." Gene looked up at Miles. "Might as well start getting used to the idea." Gene returned an uncertain smile.

Chapter 12

Gene stood in front of the mirror in his cramped bathroom. He stared at his reflection for a long while, paying close attention to all the details of his face—the shape of his nose, the angle of his jawline, the deep brown color of his eyes. He studied it intensely, leaning in as close to the mirror as he could.

"Yo, Gene, you here?" Mike called out.

"In the bathroom!"

Mike peered around the corner and found Gene with his face nearly touching the mirror glass.

"What are you doing?"

"Looking for someone."

"In the mirror?"

Gene sighed and took a step back. "You remember that guy I told you about last night?"

"You mean that guy that gave you the money?"

"Yeah, him, his name is Miles Sharpe."

"What about him?"

"He offered me a recording contract."

"You're shittin' me."

"I signed with his management company this morning."

"Congrats, man!" They shook hands.

"Thanks." Gene leaned in toward the mirror again. "He said Gene Phillips could never be a rock star. He wants me to change my name."

"What's he want you to change it to?"

"Xavier Kaine."

"Xavier Kaine?" Gene looked at him. "Well, are you okay with that?"

"I haven't decided yet. I keep looking, but I just don't see him. Do you?"

Mike stood beside Gene as they stared at the reflection. "You look like Gene," Mike said after a couple of minutes.

"I know."

"Maybe if you say the name, you'll see it," Mike suggested.

"Xavier Kaine." He waited, but nothing changed. "Xavier Kaine… Xavier Kaine!" Gene rested his back against the wall behind him. "It's no use, Mike, I just don't see it. How in the hell am I going to pull this off?"

"Introduce yourself to me."

"What?"

"Just do it," Mike said. He stuck out his hand. "I'm Mike."

Gene shook his friend's hand. "I'm Gene."

"No, no, no, say the new name! Hi, I'm Mike."

"Hi, I'm Gene… I mean, Xavier… this is stupid!"

"Come on, try it again." He stuck his hand out a third time. "Hi, I'm Mike." Gene stared at him; Mike urged him on.

"Hi, I'm Xavier Kaine," he stated in a monotone voice.

"Well, at least you got the name right that time. Say it again."

"Hi, I'm Xavier Kaine."

"Good, now say it to him," Mike instructed as he pointed to Gene's reflection.

"Hi, I'm Xavier Kaine."

"Again."

"Mike…"

"Say it! I'm Xavier Kaine!"

Gene sighed. "I'm Xavier Kaine."

"Again."

"I'm Xavier Kaine."

"Again!"

"I'm Xavier Kaine… I'm Xavier Kaine… I'm Xavier Kaine… I'm Xavier Kaine… I'm Xavier Kaine… I'm Xavier Kaine…*I'm Xavier Kaine!*"

Gene stared hard at the reflection, straightened his shoulders and stood as tall as he could. He turned to face his friend.

"Hi, I'm Mike." He extended his hand and Gene shook it firmly.

"Hello, I'm Xavier Kaine."

The two men looked into the mirror; Mike smiled.

"Hello, Xavier, it's nice to meet you."

Chapter 13

Gene entered the deli and saw its owner near the back. He set his instrument aside and moved closer.

"Hey Eddie?"

"Yeah?"

"Got a minute?"

Eddie looked up and smiled. "For you? I got all night! Lock the door and flip the sign."

Eddie went behind the counter and retrieved their usual fare—deli sandwiches, chips and sodas—then joined Gene at the small table.

"What can I do for you, Gene?"

"Nothing really, I just wanted to say goodbye."

"You're leaving?" Gene nodded. "Where are you off to?"

"I'm going on tour."

"Say what?" Eddie's confused expression made Gene laugh.

"I signed a recording contract. I'm going on tour."

"No foolin'?" Gene shook his head and smiled. "Congratulations!" Eddie stood from his seat and took Gene up in a firm embrace.

"Thanks!"

"I told you it would happen! Didn't I tell you?!"

"You did, and you were right!"

"So, when are you leaving?"

"In two weeks."

Eddie sat down slowly in his chair. "That soon?" Gene confirmed the statement. "Well, at least we have two more weeks."

"Actually, they want to get started right away. I'm going in the studio to record a new single and they've scheduled rehearsals and wardrobe fittings, and all these other things that have to be done before we leave. That's why I wanted to talk to you, today's my last day."

"Oh…"

"I'm sorry, Eddie."

"There's no need to apologize. This is what you came here for, this is your dream. You do what you have to do. You're gonna be hard to replace, but there are plenty of kids in this city looking for a place to play. I'm sure I'll find someone."

"That's another thing I wanted to talk to you about. I have a friend who plays the sax. He's a great guy and a great musician. I thought maybe he could take my spot out front... that is, if it's okay with you."

"Tell him to come by in the morning and we'll give it a try."

"I will, thanks!"

Gene took a bite of his sandwich and sat back in his chair. His eyes moved slowly around the interior of the building, his mind recording all the details and nuances of the deli as Eddie watched him.

"Whatcha thinkin' about, Gene?"

"All the nights we spent sitting here like this, eating sandwiches, talking... I'm really gonna miss all this." Eddie gave him a soft smile. "I'm really gonna miss you, Eddie."

"I'm gonna miss you, too."

The friends ate and talked into the wee hours, recalling memories of their two years together and their thoughts about the new life Gene would soon be embarking on. During a lull in the conversation, Eddie glanced at his watch.

"I assume you have somewhere you have to be in the morning?"

"Yeah, I do."

"I guess we'd better call it a night then."

After a quick cleanup, they shut off the lights and left the store; Eddie pulled down the security gate and locked it in place.

"Come on, I'll drive you home."

"I don't want you to go out of your way, I can take the bus..."

"At this hour? Get in the car."

Along the way, Gene watched the now familiar cityscape as it rushed past. It wouldn't be long before he would leave this place and its people behind. He knew he would be leaving a piece of himself behind as well.

Eddie pulled up along the curb in front of the building. "Well, here ya go, home sweet home."

Gene looked up at the building and sighed, then exited the car. Eddie stepped out and retrieved Gene's amp from the back seat, then met Gene as he came around to the sidewalk with his guitar; he handed the amp to Gene.

"Tomorrow starts a whole new life for you." Gene gave him half a smile. "Knock 'em dead, kid!" Eddie moved toward the car.

"Eddie?"

The man looked back at him. "Yeah, Gene?"

Gene sat down on the steps of the apartment building. He wiped his nose on his coat sleeve and looked down at the sidewalk. Eddie sat down beside him.

"You're scared?"

"Everything's changing."

"For the better, Gene, it's changing for the better."

"I know that, Eddie, but I still feel like I'm losing everything…"

"You're not losing, you're gaining. Think of the things you'll get to do, the places you'll travel to, all the music you're gonna make!"

"But I'm leaving all my friends behind."

"You'll make new friends." Gene swiped his tears away. "Nothing stays the same, Gene, everything changes. You have to do this… you were *born* to do this. This is your chance, and you have to take it!" Eddie gave Gene's shoulder a squeeze as he stood from the step. "I gotta get home," he said as he walked to the car.

"Eddie?"

"Yeah, Gene?"

"None of this would've happened without you." Eddie glanced back at the young man. Gene stood and moved toward him. "Thank you."

"Anytime, kid," Eddie said as they embraced, "anytime."

Eddie got in the car, waved and drove away. Gene watched as the car's taillights faded into the blackness, then picked up his equipment and went inside.

He stood in the large foyer letting his senses absorb all the familiar sights and sounds. He had made this place his home for the last couple of years. He had gotten to know many of the tenants and considered them friends. In two short weeks, he would be gone, but he knew he would never forget them. They had made an indelible impression on his life. He hoped he had done the same for them. Gene climbed the steps to his apartment, went in and tried his best to get some sleep.

## Chapter 14

Miles buzzed his secretary and had her send for Richard Long, a young man from the Sharpe Management Artists & Repertoire department. Richard had been with the company for the past two years, brown-nosing his way through the ranks and trying to make it into Miles Sharpe's band of senior associates, the ones with lots of special perks and six-figure salaries. He was eager to please and exactly the type of person Miles needed.

Richard knocked on the door and poked his head in. Miles was standing behind his desk going through various piles of paperwork.

"You wanted to see me, Mr. Sharpe?

"Yes, Richard, come in," he answered without looking up, motioning with his hands still full of papers, "close the door and take a seat."

Richard sat down in one of the chairs in front of Miles' desk and waited patiently while his boss finished sorting through the stacks of forms. Afterward, he placed one of the stacks into a manila envelope, then sat down and looked at Richard. Neither of them spoke for several seconds and Richard became uncomfortable.

"Can I get you anything, sir?"

"No." He continued to stare; Richard grew uneasy.

"Did I do something wrong?"

"Why would you think that?"

Richard gave half a shrug. "Deductive reasoning. If you don't need anything, then you must want to talk to me about something I did wrong."

"I did want to talk to you about your job…"

"Am I not performing my duties to your satisfaction, sir?"

"On the contrary, your work has been exemplary. You work harder and put in more hours than most of my staff. You may even spend more time here than I do!" The two men shared a laugh and Richard began to relax.

"Thank you, sir. It's a relief to know that I have met your expectations of my abilities."

"Exceeded, Richard," Miles corrected him, "you've exceeded my expectations."

"That's quite a compliment, sir, thank you. May I ask then, what it was you wanted to see me about?"

"Richard, I have a proposal for you. I'm sure by now you've heard that we've signed a very promising new artist."

"You mean Xavier Kaine?"

"Correct. Mr. Kaine will be going out on tour in the very near future and he's going to need someone to act as his personal assistant, someone to take care of him, make sure his needs are met. I want you to be that someone, Richard."

"*Me*, Mr. Sharpe? Are you sure?"

"Yes, Richard, I want you."

"Well of course, I'd be honored, but…"

"Excellent! Here, take this home and study it." He shoved the manila envelope in Richard's direction.

"What is it?" Richard asked as he opened the flap and removed the papers.

"It's everything you need to know about Xavier Kaine. I want you to know all of that by the time we leave. Read it, study it, consume it… *digest it*. It should be part of your natural thinking process."

"Favorite color, favorite foods, shirt size, pant size, shoe size, favorite TV shows, *preferred female type*? Forgive me, sir, but what does all this have to do with being Mr. Kaine's personal assistant? Shouldn't I be handling more important matters like hotel reservations, security issues…"

"That's already been taken care of."

"But…"

"Richard, from this point on, the entire focus of your career will be about keeping Xavier Kaine happy. If Xavier Kaine is happy, then his fans will be happy, and those fans will go out and spend their money on Xavier Kaine merchandise, which means more profit for the company. That will make me happy and I can then write you a nice fat paycheck which, I assume, will make you ecstatic."

"Yes sir."

"Now, if Xavier Kaine is unhappy, then his fans will be unhappy, and they won't buy Xavier Kaine merchandise, and so on and so on… do you see where I'm going with this?"

"Yes sir."

Miles took Richard by the elbow and led him toward the door. "Good, now go get started and we'll talk more later." He opened the door, but Richard paused.

"Mr. Sharpe?"

"Yes, Richard?"

"I'm sorry, but I'm still a little confused."

"About what?"

"About why you chose me for this position."

"You don't think you're qualified?"

"No sir, I believe I'm *over-qualified*. I've been here longer than most of the people in my department, I'm also one of the highest paid. I'm just wondering why you would choose someone at my level to be a glorified gopher for Mr. Kaine when you could get one of the entry-level people to do it for half the amount I make."

Miles studied him a moment. He had been watching how Richard interacted with the other members of the staff and evaluating how he conducted himself with clients. He knew Richard wanted to be one of Miles' chosen few, the 'Golden Circle', as the those in the lower levels had dubbed it. He wanted it so badly that he salivated just being in Miles' office, but he still had the balls to question the CEO's decision to give him the job. He was a brave son-of-a-bitch, Miles had to give him credit for that, and he had underestimated the boy's intellect. When he decided to offer Richard the job as Xavier's assistant, he assumed the young man would jump at the chance without question. Obviously, he had assumed wrong, and now he had to do a little tap dancing.

Miles smiled as he walked over to the sideboard by the window and poured himself a scotch. "Would you like something?" he offered.

"No, thank you."

Miles sat back against the edge of the sideboard and took a sip of his drink. "Richard, you're right. You are absolutely, unequivocally correct. I could hire someone from the ground floor to do everything for Mr. Kaine that I'm asking you to do for much less than your current salary, and they would be thrilled to do it."

"So why don't you?"

"Did you ever hear the phrase, 'You get what you pay for'?" Richard nodded. "You see, I could hire one of those entry-level people for half the salary, but I would also get *half* the experience and *half* the knowledge that you've gained through the two years that you've worked for me. I've had my eye on you for a while now, Richard…"

"You have, sir?"

"Yes, I have. I've heard people complaining about how you're always trying to outdo everyone, how you're always pestering your supervisors with annoying questions and how you're making everyone else look bad to the boss, but that's what *they* see. Let me tell you what *I* see. I see a young man who does what needs to be done and puts in the extra hours to get the job finished on time. I see a young man with an extraordinary attention to detail and a keen sense of intuition. I see a young man who is secure and confident in his ability to accomplish the tasks he was assigned, who won't let anyone else's issues get in his way.

"Sure, I could get some flunky kiss-ass or some magna cum laude who thinks he's entitled, but that's not what I want. I want someone who cares, someone who gives a damn. I want someone who'll look out for the company's assets, someone who'll report directly to me, to be my second in command, so to speak." Miles guided Richard to sit in one of the chairs in front of his desk; he sat in the other. He looked into Richard's eyes with a softened expression. "Xavier Kaine is special, he's a one-of-a-kind performer. You've heard him play."

"Yes sir, he's incredible."

"Yes, he is, he is *incredible*! I can't leave him in the hands of some grunt who just arrived, someone *that* special, someone *that* incredible needs someone equally incredible to take care of them. That's you, Richard. Xavier Kaine *needs you*!"

Richard considered the man's explanation. "I understand now, Mr. Sharpe, thank you. I can see that you have Mr. Kaine's best interests at heart."

"Yes, Richard, I do."

"I'll know this information inside out by the time the tour starts," Richard told him as he stood and started for the door.

"I knew I could count on you, Richard!"

He stopped at the door. "Thank you for this opportunity, Mr. Sharpe, you won't regret it!"

As Richard left the office, Miles sat back in the chair and raised his glass. "Oscar-winning performance, Mr. Sharpe, bravo!" He laughed and finished off the glass of scotch.

## Chapter 15

Gene lay in his makeshift bed watching as the new day ushered out the night sky. Sleep had eluded him, his mind still trying to comprehend all that was happening to him. After playing his guitar on the sidewalk through two years of scorching hot summers and freezing winters, the 'right' person finally heard his music. Miles Sharpe opened a door for him; Gene took a chance and walked through. Once he stepped over that threshold, his life began, and it was no dream. This time it was for real, and there was no turning back.

He sat up, rubbing his weary eyes, and pulled his wallet from the back pocket of his jeans. He opened it to the photo insert and flipped the small pages until he came to a photo of his mom and dad.

Gene stared at the picture. He wanted to call his parents and tell them about everything he had done over the last two years. He wanted to tell them about his crappy little apartment and his friend, Mike; about Eddie and playing in front of the deli. He wanted to call them and tell them he had finally made it. He wanted to, but he couldn't. They hadn't spoken since he left home, so he was sure there would be hard feelings among them. Gene felt a twinge of remorse and quickly closed the wallet.

His thoughts moved back to the day at hand, and he glanced at his watch. The morning had barely begun, but he knew Mike would be awake. This would be Gene's only chance to talk to him before leaving for the tour.

After dressing and freshening up, Gene grabbed two six-packs of beer and went a couple doors down the hallway; he knocked on Mike's door. When his friend answered, Gene held up the first six-pack.

"What's this?" Mike asked.

"A thank-you gift, for being such a great friend."

Mike laughed as he took the beer and placed it in the fridge. He turned to see Gene holding up the other six-pack.

"And this is?"

"A goodbye gift."

Mike sighed. "You're really goin', huh?" Gene nodded and Mike placed the beer in the fridge with the first pack.

"It won't be as much fun without you."

Mike smiled. "You bet your ass, it won't!"

Gene laughed, knowing Mike was trying to lighten to mood, and for a minute, he had succeeded. The jovial mood soon faded, and the gravity of the situation hung heavy between them.

"Come with me, Mike."

The man shook his head. "No, Gene…"

"I'll clear it with Miles. You deserve this chance as much as I do."

"This is your chance, Gene, not mine. I don't want to ride on your coattails."

"But you wouldn't be! You're a skilled musician, Mike. We could play as a duo!"

"Sure Gene, we could be a duo."

Mike opened his horn case on the table and took out the saxophone. After attaching a new reed to the reed table, he applied cork grease to the neck of the instrument and spread it around with his finger. Gene watched as his friend gently twisted the mouthpiece in place and attached the neck to the horn body.

"I gotta go." Gene waited, but Mike didn't respond. "See ya, Mike."

"See ya, Gene," Mike said, his back to his friend. He wiped the sax with a cleaning cloth, then raised the mouthpiece to his lips and played an up-tempo jazz number.

Gene removed an envelope from his pocket and laid it on top of the open case, then went to the door. After one last glance over his shoulder, he left the apartment. When Mike heard the door shut, he stopped playing. He listened as Gene's footsteps faded to silence. Tears dripped down Mike's cheeks and he wiped them away. He attempted to go back to playing, but the feeling had left him.

Mike went back to the table and started to disassemble the instrument, then noticed the white envelope Gene had left for him. He unclipped the neck strap from the ring on the sax and laid the horn aside; then opened the envelope:

Dear Mike,

As I expected, you turned down my invitation to join me on tour. I wish you would have accepted; we would have killed it onstage together!

I know I said this already, but I feel the need to say it again. Thank you for being such a great friend. It's because of you that I was able to survive those first few months. I wouldn't be going on tour now if I hadn't met you that first day. Your friendship means everything to me.

Enclosed with this letter, you'll find a debit card with your name on it. I have added you to my account at National Bank & Trust as an authorized user. Take as much as you need for whatever you need.

I hope someday you'll change your mind and join me on the road. Until then, please take care of yourself, Mike.

Forever your friend,

Gene

Mike laid the letter on the table, then walked to the refrigerator and pulled two bottles of beer from one of the cartons. He unscrewed the caps from both bottles and set one in front of the empty chair beside him. As he stared at his name printed in gold across the front of the bank card, his emotions returned. Mike tapped his bottle against the one next to him.

"Forever friends," he toasted. He tipped the bottle back and drank it down.

# THE TOUR

Chapter 16

The security guards battled a path through the clusters of stagehands, arena personnel and paparazzi until they reached the far end of the hallway. On the nondescript door hung a gold star with 'XAVIER KAINE' emblazoned in its center.

Xavier entered the room and went directly to a rectangular table that sat along a far wall. He laid his guitar case out flat on the table top and pulled a soft white towel from inside, using it to wipe the sweat and skin oil from the instrument. When he was satisfied with its cleanliness, Xavier rested the guitar inside the hard-shell case, like a mother would lay her baby in its crib; he secured the lid.

"Xavier." He turned to see Miles with his arm extended holding a short crystal tumbler filled with ice cubes and whiskey. Richard transferred the glass from Miles' hand to Xavier's. Miles raised his glass and grinned. "To success!"

"To success!" the other men repeated in unison. Xavier, still drenched in sweat from the show, plopped into a cushy chair, propped his feet on the coffee table and laid his head back.

"I think we can now say that Xavier Kaine has been officially launched," Miles commented.

"What a show!" Richard said as he bounced around the dressing room like an agitated chihuahua. "You were *fantastic*, X!"

Xavier stared at the ceiling and shook his head. "It can't possibly get any better than this."

"Oh, but it can, my friend, and it will." Miles walked over and stood behind Xavier's chair. "You are on the verge of becoming an international superstar."

"Come on, Miles…"

"Trust me, before you know it every female with an active libido will be drooling at the mention of your name. You'll be everywhere—newspapers, magazines, television, radio—*and* you'll be trending on every social media site on the internet. Young man, *you* are about to become the brightest star in the universe!" Xavier stared up at him, unconvinced.

"I gotta take care of some business, but I'll be back. You just sit here and relax, you've earned it." He raised his glass high as he walked to the door. "All hail Xavier Kaine!" he declared before finishing off the whiskey. He set the glass aside on his way out.

Xavier closed his eyes and tried to wrap his mind around what Miles had just told him. Every dream he had for himself was coming true, and it was happening fast. Less than two years prior, he had been playing on the street; living off tips and Eddie's deli sandwiches. Now, he plays to audiences of thousands, he stays in the most expensive hotels and travels by limousine and private jet. Maybe Miles was right, maybe the best was yet to come.

"Did you see those girls?" Richard asked as he returned from refilling his drink.

"You mean the ones in front of the stage that flashed me? Yeah, I saw them," he answered with a laugh.

"Man, they wanted you bad!" Richard paused to take a sip of his whiskey. "I could get you one."

"One what?"

"One of those girls."

Xavier gave him a sideways glance. "How?"

"Invite them to dinner."

"You think they'd actually come with you?"

"If I invite them to have dinner with Xavier Kaine? In a heartbeat!"

"A lot of those girls are really young, Richard. We'd be taking a huge chance…"

"Don't worry, I'll handle everything."

"But how will you know who to invite?"

"You'll tell me."

"*I'll* tell you?" Xavier asked, his eyebrows raised.

"The next time we do a show, you pick out the one you like and send me a signal."

"What kind of signal?"

"I don't know, a nod or something, then after the show, I'll go talk to her."

They sat staring at each other for several seconds. Finally, Xavier laughed and shook his head.

"This is a crazy idea, Richard!"

"But it'll work!" the assistant said with a wide grin. He held his glass in the air. "All hail Xavier Kaine!"

Xavier smiled as he raised his glass and tapped it against Richard's. "To success!"

Chapter 17

Xavier stepped through the door and closed it, locking the deadbolt. He placed his guitar in its case, then dabbed at his face with the towel that hung around his neck. He headed to the sofa, laid down and closed his eyes. Several moments later, he heard a muffled rattling above him. He peered up, his sight blurry from a combination of exhaustion and perspiration, to see a glint of reflected light. He heard the rattling sound again as the shiny object moved in a quick back-and-forth motion. He tried to focus as he reached up toward the glare and grasping the object in his palm, he pulled it toward him. A mysterious woman stared down at him.

"Great show tonight, Xavier," she commented as she walked back to the bar. Xavier rolled over, leaned on one elbow and examined the glass, sniffing its contents. He took a swallow of the brown liquid. "You're very talented."

"Thanks," he replied, sitting up on the edge of the sofa. He turned to face her. "I'm sorry, have we met before?"

"No."

He stood up, assuming a defensive posture. "Then who are you? And how the hell did you get in here?!"

"Relax, I'm not a threat," she answered. He took in several details about her as she moved across the room and sat down on the sofa. She was older than him—though not by more than a decade or so—and was a striking woman with lustrous auburn tresses surrounding a face that had a slight curve at the jawline. Almond-shaped viridescent eyes, a perfectly proportioned nose, and lips that made his mouth water completed the living portrait that sat before him. "Let's just say I'm a friend of a friend. Sit down, have a drink with me. Let's get to know each other a little better." She smiled and patted the sofa cushion beside her.

Xavier tossed back what remained in the glass and went back to the bar for a refill. The woman waited for him to respond.

"Who are you a friend of?" he asked, their backs to each other.

"Does it matter?"

"Yeah, it does."

"What are you going to do, fire them?" She glanced backward over her shoulder; Xavier didn't turn around. The woman stood and walked to the bar. "Don't get so worked up about it, Xavier," she said, rubbing her hand across his back.

He turned and took her by the arm. "You have to leave," he said, leading her to the door.

"Why?"

"I have to shower and change…"

"Go ahead, I've seen a naked man before," she told him with a laugh and a smile. He sighed and rolled his eyes. "Are you shy?" Xavier gave her an annoyed glance, unbolted the lock and opened the door, but the woman shoved it closed just as fast. He turned and leaned back against the wall. "Are you a virgin, Xavier?" He said nothing, his eyes fixed on hers. "It's okay if you are, you know. To be honest, I find it quite titillating. I enjoy being able to school a young man on the many ways to truly pleasure a woman."

Stepping closer to him, she drew her left palm across the bulge in the front of his tight jeans and grasped his member. His eyes left hers for just a moment as he glanced down. She smiled as he leaned in to kiss her, his mouth opening, his tongue reaching deep to find hers. He pulled her closer, pressing her body against his own. She gasped for breath as his teeth nipped at the skin on her neck.

Xavier stood straight and looked into her eyes. He watched as she ran the tip of her middle finger slowly over the firm flesh of his pectoral muscles, his sweat accumulating on its tip, then placed the finger in her mouth and sucked off the taste of him.

"Richard!" Xavier yelled out, banging his fist on the dressing room door.

Richard turned the knob and peeked through the small opening. "You need something, X?"

"Escort Ms…" He paused.

"Devon, Natalia Devon."

"Escort Ms. Devon to my limo, she'll be accompanying me to the hotel," he instructed, his brown eyes never leaving her gaze.

"Sure thing, X," the assistant answered, "Right this way, Ms. Devon."

Natalia's left hand gave a slight squeeze as she smiled at Xavier and left the dressing room. He stood a moment, then locked the door and headed for the shower, grabbing his drink from the bar as he passed.

Plumbs of steam rose up around him as he washed and stood under the showerhead, letting the water rinse the soap suds away. His eyes followed the drops as they ran down his torso, joining and forming tiny streams that flowed along the curves of his muscles. He tried to clear his mind, tried to relax, but it was no use, she wouldn't let him.

*Natalia Devon...* The very thought of her name aroused him. The way she spoke to him, the way she touched him had awakened something inside him. Was he a virgin? Yes, she had guessed correctly, but he wasn't about to admit it. He felt the blood rush to his pelvis and watched as his manhood became erect, the folds of skin smoothing as it lengthened.

*Natalia Devon...* He reached down and rubbed his groin, gently massaging his testes each time his hand neared them...

*Natalia Devon...* He closed his eyes as his hand slid up to his shaft and he slowly stroked out and back... out and back... out and back...

*Natalia Devon!* He strengthened his grip, stroking harder and faster, harder and faster, harder and faster...

*Natalia Devon!!* His leg muscles tensed; he slammed a hand against the wall of the shower to brace himself...

*NATALIA DEVON!!!* He felt his glutes contract as the orgasm took command of him; he groaned loud and deep...

**"*UUUUUUUUUNNNNNNNNNNNNNHHHHHHHHHH!!*"**

Xavier stood with his forehead against the shower wall, breathless, his heart pounding, his nerve endings so alive that every drop of water made his skin prickle.

He turned his face up toward the showerhead for a few moments before turning the knobs off. He dried and dressed, then grabbed some personal items and his guitar; he opened the door.

"Let's go!" Xavier said as he passed by his assistant, nearly knocking him into the wall.

Richard pulled himself together as he and several security guards followed Xavier out to the waiting limousine.

## Chapter 18

Richard knocked on the door of the hotel suite, then inserted his keycard and stepped in. Xavier was seated on the sofa with his head in his hands. Richard could see the man's body trembling.

"You okay, X?" Xavier didn't look up. "I was thinking about ordering some dinner. You want something?" He waited, but Xavier said nothing. "X?" He watched as Xavier began to slowly rock back and forth. Richard sat down on the edge of the coffee table, facing him. "How about I just get you a dessert?"

"No," the man grumbled.

"Come on, X…"

"I'm not hungry, Richard!" Xavier stood and moved to the window, rubbing his hands through his sweaty hair.

"You need to eat…"

"I'll eat when I'm hungry!"

"Why don't you go to bed then? I'll make sure no one bothers you."

"I'm too wired."

Richard walked over to the window, pulled a small metal box from his pocket and offered a sample to him.

"Here."

Xavier turned and saw a small, round white pill in Richard's palm. "I told you before, I don't want any pills."

"It won't hurt you; it'll just make you drowsy."

"I said no!"

"Xavier, you haven't slept in *three days*! You have a show tomorrow night, you have to get some rest!" Richard poured some wine from a bottle on the bar and held out his hands to the man, wine glass in one, the pill in the other. "Would you rather read in the papers about how you passed out on stage from exhaustion?"

Xavier looked at him again and Richard stretched his hands out closer to the musician. Xavier took the items and held the pill between his finger and thumb, staring at it.

"It's legit, I promise. I got it from my doctor, it's my own prescription. I take them myself when I can't sleep." Richard paused. "Honestly, I have the bottle in my room. You can trust me, X, I would never give you anything that would hurt you." He paused a second time. He could tell his boss was still undecided. "You want to sleep, don't you?"

He glanced at Richard, who gave him a sympathetic smile. Xavier didn't like the idea of relying on medication, but Richard did have a point. This insomnia showed no signs of letting him be and if he didn't get some sleep soon, the show would suffer for it. He sighed, tossed the pill into his mouth and washed it down with the contents of the wine glass.

"Now just go in the bedroom and crash for a few hours," Richard said as he took the wine glass from Xavier's hand and guided him toward the doorway. "Don't worry, if anything comes up, I'll handle it."

Xavier stepped over the threshold and Richard closed the door between them.


Xavier stood just inside the bedroom. With the door closed, the well-insulated walls kept the room quiet and peaceful. It was a welcome relief to his over-stimulated senses. Night after night, his eyes were filled with pulsating stage lights, camera flashes and a never-ending sea of faces; his ears bombarded by pounding drums, screeching guitars and legions of screaming fans. He had almost forgotten what silent solitude felt like.

He peeled off his sweaty clothes on the way to the bed, letting the items fall in a wrinkled trail as he walked. He moved the blankets and crawled into the coolness of the fresh sheets, his muscles giving way to the fatigue as his head sunk into the softness of the pillow. Xavier gathered the blankets around him, only to kick them off again a minute later, stretching his long, nude body down the length of the king-sized mattress. He shivered now and then as the chilled air from the hotel's cooling system blew across his skin.

As he lay in a supine position staring at the ceiling, waiting for the medicine to take effect, his thoughts carried him back to the farm where he was raised. He could smell the hay bales they kept stacked in the barn and the fragrant scent of the wildflowers that grew in the fields all around the house. He could see the moonbeams that danced with the rippling curtains every time the cool night breeze blew through his open bedroom window. He remembered how hard he and his father worked to keep the farm going, and how tired he always was at the end of the day. Sleeping had never been a problem then, since his exhausted body could literally do nothing else.

Xavier closed his eyes. Off in the distance, he could hear what sounded like a female voice. It drew closer and closer until he could see the woman's face; it was his mother. He remembered how she would hug him close and kiss him on the cheek every night before he went to bed.

*"Goodnight, Eugene, I love you…"*

A faint smile crossed his weary face. "Night, Mom… love you, too…" he replied in a hushed voice as he drifted off.

Miles slipped the keycard into the slot and opened the door to Xavier's hotel suite. As he stepped in, he saw Richard sitting alone at the table enjoying the steak and lobster dinner he had ordered from room service.

"Where is he?" Richard tilted his head toward the bedroom. "He finally went to sleep?"

"He had a little help from my friends," he told Miles as he shook the metal pill box, the pills rattling inside.

Miles smirked. "One pill makes you larger and one pill makes you small." The two men laughed at the song reference.

"Any particular time you need him to get up?" Richard asked as he chewed.

"No, let him sleep. I need him to be ready to go in the morning. Call me if there's any problems."

"What if he wakes up before morning?"

Miles looked at him and shrugged. "Introduce him to another one of your 'friends'."

Miles headed out of the suite, leaving the assistant alone with his dinner. Richard smiled and laughed to himself as he dunked a chunk of lobster in the small bowl of melted butter and placed it in his mouth.

## Chapter 19

Xavier lay naked in the bed, totally spent – his sexual escapades with Natalia always left him that way – but he was wide awake. His mind reeled with images of the tour; names, faces and cities spun through his memory like a cyclone.

Natalia stirred and moved closer to him, draping her arm across his firm abs; he rolled onto his side, his back to her. They were both still for a short while before she inched her body up against his. Xavier sighed; he pushed her arm away and slid from the bed.

He wrapped his robe around him, letting the front hang open, then picked up his guitar and sat on the ottoman. Xavier pulled his thumb lightly across the strings, playing a graceful melody. Natalia leaned on one elbow and listened for a few minutes, then left the bed and drew up behind him.

"Can't sleep?"

"No."

"Why don't you come back to bed? I'm sure we can find a way to occupy ourselves." She ran her fingers through his hair; he brushed them away.

"I'm not in the mood."

"I can help with that, too."

Natalia laid her body across his shoulders and kissed his neck, her hands roaming over the skin on his torso. Xavier stood and moved to the sofa in the next room, then went back to the song he was playing. Natalia stood bare in the doorway of the bedroom. Her thirst for him was so great, it threatened to consume her. She craved his touch; to taste his mouth on hers; she was desperate to feel him inside her.

There may be other women in his life, but they were no competition. Everything Xavier did to please them, he learned from her. He may like to flit around with the worker bees, but Natalia was the queen, and she ruled the hive. Xavier Kaine belonged to her.

## Chapter 20

The tour had been extended a third time, which meant Xavier had little more than a week off before heading back out on the road again. Response for his debut album had been phenomenal and more and more venues wanted to book him for concerts. New cities were added to the schedule on an almost daily basis, and tickets were selling out within hours of going on sale.

The limo pulled into the lot behind the arena and stopped close to the building. The chauffer opened the back door; Richard stepped out and glanced around at the enormous gathering of fans.

"This is insane!" he commented as Miles exited the car.

"This is perfection!" Miles replied with a wide grin. He stepped aside as Xavier emerged.

A deafening wave of sound came at them from the cheering crowd when they saw their hero. Xavier savored their praise, smiling and waving as they called out to him. He took his time following the path that had been set up for their arrival while strings of patrol officers did their best to keep the fans at bay. The paparazzi were just as enthusiastic, with blinding lights at every turn and questions being rapid fired at the star.

Xavier stopped, focusing on a young woman near the front of the crowd. He moved in her direction, his eyes drinking in her loveliness. The crowd became quiet; they waited and watched. Xavier reached up and caressed her cheek.

"You're very beautiful," he told her as he moved a few stray strands of her blondish-brown hair from her face, "May I kiss you?" She stood entranced as the singer leaned in and gently pressed his mouth to hers. Xavier held her head in his hands as the kiss deepened and she gave in to him, letting his tongue wrap around hers. The release was slow and easy as he pulled back from her, licked his lips and smiled. As the entourage proceeded onward toward the stage entrance, Xavier blew a kiss to the young fan, then glanced over his shoulder at his assistant.

## Chapter 21

Richard arrived back at the hotel shortly after Xavier and escorted the 'dinner date' into the suite.

"Have a seat, Xavier will be out in a minute." The girl sat down in an armchair near the sofa. "Would you like a drink?"

"No, thank you," she answered in a shy voice.

"Are you sure? I could make you a martini…"

"Don't pester the lady, Richard. I'd like a rum and Coke," Xavier said. He turned to his guest. "Would you like a soda?"

"Can I have a rum and Coke?"

Xavier smiled at her. "Make that two, Richard."

"Sure thing Boss!"

Xavier carried the drinks over to the sofa. "Would you care to join me?" He waited until the young woman had seated herself before sitting on the cushion beside her.

"Thank you," she said, taking the glass from Xavier's hand.

"Cheers!" he toasted, tapping his glass to hers. They sipped at the drinks, and she coughed, the strong taste of the rum catching in her throat.

"Are you all right?"

"Mmmhmm…"

"Do you want some water?"

"No," she answered, clearing her throat, "I'm fine, thank you." She sipped again from the tumbler and smiled.

Richard seated himself in the armchair and nursed his cocktail while Xavier and his guest chatted. He had witnessed this scenario many times in many cities throughout the tour. Xavier would choose a young lady from the crowd and signal to Richard by blowing the woman a kiss. Richard would search her out after the show and tell her Xavier would like to invite her to dinner, if she was interested. Of course, they were *always* interested, and Richard would make all the necessary arrangements.

As he listened to their conversation, Richard felt envious toward Xavier's female acquaintance. As his friend and confidant, as the person Xavier relied on, he had a special relationship with the star, but it wasn't quite the same as what the man shared with the women Richard brought to him.

Xavier shared an intimacy with them that Richard found himself craving. He couldn't help his attraction. Xavier was tall and tan, with a young, firm body and a presence that couldn't be denied. When he took the stage, he owned it. He was larger than life and his fans loved every minute of the experience.

Richard watched the two as they conversed, Xavier complimenting her and the young woman swooning over him. He watched Xavier's lips as they moved, his voice smooth and rich, commanding and irresistible... he would do anything Xavier Kaine asked of him... *absolutely anything*...

"Richard?" Xavier tossed a small pillow at him to get his attention. "Richard!"

The assistant jumped, embarrassed to be caught daydreaming. "Sorry X, did you need something?"

"Dinner would be nice."

"Dinner, of course, I'll have them bring it right up!" Richard went to the phone and verified that room service was on their way. Afterward, he excused himself and returned to his own hotel room.

He ran a shower and stood under the water, but he couldn't get Xavier Kaine out of his senses. His desire was too strong for him to overcome. Richard hadn't intended for this to happen, he hadn't intended to fall in love, yet that's exactly where he found himself. He was completely devoted to a man he could never have.

As the water washed over him, Richard thought about the woman Xavier was with. He thought about what Xavier was saying to her, what they might be doing at that moment. He thought about how Xavier would kiss her, touch her... make love to her. She was beautiful—all the women Xavier shared himself with were beautiful...and Richard hated them all.

Once dinner was finished, Xavier sat admiring the girl across from him. Here in the warm glow of the lamplight, she was even more alluring than when he had first seen her before the show. She wasn't very old, but she was old enough, and he couldn't wait to taste her.

"Do you like to dance?" he asked. She nodded, and Xavier stood from the table. He switched on some soft music and took his date in his arms. They danced slow and close, Xavier's face looking straight into hers. He kissed her again as he had kissed her before, his need growing stronger, his desire more intense. He spun her around to face away from him and pulled her close as they continued their rhythmic sway.

Xavier leaned in and pressed his lips tenderly to the girl's shoulder, following it until he reached the natural curve of her neck. He noticed that she tasted faintly of vanilla and strawberries, and he could see the nerves just below the surface of her barely-legal flesh quiver at his touch.

She was a virgin, he could tell; he'd had her kind before. They always reacted the same way—pretending to know the score but scared totally shitless inside. He found their lack of experience enticing. Their naivety made them easy to impress, and since they were so willing to please him, they never questioned his requests.

Xavier felt the familiar craving building inside him, and he smiled. What was her name again? He couldn't remember. It didn't matter anyway. He didn't plan on ever seeing her again. His long arms wound around her like the tendrils of a vine, slithering their way into places they were never meant to go.

"Mr. Kaine are you sure we should be doing this?" she asked.

He turned her around to face him.

"Say my name," his deep voice implored.

"Xavier…"

"Slower," he instructed, his face now only inches away from hers.

"Xavier…" she repeated in a slow breathy whisper.

He exhaled heavily and looked into her eyes as his hand found its way to the hem of her miniskirt; he inched it higher up her thigh.

"Do you want me to make love to you?"

"Yes."

"Yes what?"

"Yes, Xavier…"

Chapter 22

Xavier and Richard moved around the hotel suite gathering Xavier's belongings and cramming them into suitcases. After a short while, Xavier sat down on the end of the bed.

"Jesus, I'm tired," he said as he fell back onto the mattress, "Why can't we just stay here for another week?" Richard stopped packing and sat down next to Xavier. He heaved a sigh as he glanced at the bulky suitcases, remembering all the times they had been packed and unpacked.

"We could talk to Miles."

"About what?"

"About a break."

Xavier sat up on his elbows and looked at his assistant. "He'd never go for it."

"You'll never know unless you ask him."

"Why aren't you ready to go?" The two men turned to see Miles standing in the bedroom doorway.

"Miles, Xavier wanted to ask you a question."

"Richard!" Xavier gave him a stern look.

"We don't have time for games, Richard," Miles said.

"Ask him, X!" Xavier shook his head.

"Ask me what?!"

"Miles, X was wondering if we could maybe fit a short hiatus into the schedule."

"A hiatus? We can't take a hiatus now; the schedule is full."

"I know, but maybe after these dates we could slow down a little, you know, maybe not schedule the shows so close together so X can have a few days to rest in between..."

"No problem, Richard, I'll just tell the venues that they'll have to rearrange their entire schedule, so Xavier Kaine can get his beauty sleep before his next show!"

"I need a break, Miles!"

"We can't take a break now! The album is soaring up the charts, the tour dates are selling out faster than we can book them... everyone wants Xavier Kaine! Stopping now would be professional suicide!!"

"But Miles..."

"It is out of the question!" Miles shouted. "Do either of you know what it takes to make this schedule happen? Do you know what it takes to not only put Xavier Kaine on the charts, but to *keep* him there?

"*I* am the one with the connections, and *I* am the one paying the bills, so *I* make the rules! *There will be no breaks in the tour schedule!!* Now both of you get your shit together, we're leaving for the airport in an hour!"

Miles slammed the door on his way out; his rant left Richard and Xavier speechless. Xavier opened one of the suitcases and went back to packing; Richard went after Miles, catching up with him at the elevator.

"Miles, he can't keep going at this pace, it's killing him! He has to rest!"

"He will rest."

"*When?*"

"When I *tell* him to!"

"That's not good enough, Miles!"

"Now you listen to me, you little shit! You're only here because I *allow* you to stay, but you could be gone in a flash, and so could Xavier Kaine."

"You *need* Xavier Kaine!"

"*I CREATED XAVIER KAINE!!* And I can do it again! You are *both* expendable, Richard. Now I suggest you get back in there and do the job I so generously pay you to do, unless you'd rather join your righteous indignation in the unemployment line. I can always find someone else to take care of your precious Xavier."

Miles stepped into the elevator; he smiled at Richard as the doors closed.

## Chapter 23

Xavier wrapped a towel around himself and left the bathroom. He gathered his clothes on his way to the living room, rubbing his wet hair with a second towel to soak up the excess moisture. Looking up, he saw Natalia Devon lounging on the sofa, her stocking feet stretched out in front of her with her ankles crossed; she smiled.

"Hello handsome."

"What are you doing here?" he asked.

"I thought I'd have dinner with you tonight."

"You should have called." He rubbed over his exposed skin with the second towel and tossed it toward the bathroom.

"That would have spoiled the surprise."

Xavier pulled on his underwear and gave the other towel a fling. "I'm busy tonight," he told her as he continued to dress.

"Busy with what… or maybe I should ask with *who*?" The man ignored her as he buttoned his shirt. "Is she one of the little flowers you picked from your garden?"

"That's none of your business." Xavier went back to the bathroom to comb his hair.

"Call them and cancel, you're spending tonight with me."

"No," he answered as he returned from the bathroom.

"I have the whole night planned out; you don't have to do a thing… at least, not until we get back to the hotel."

"I told you, *I'm busy*."

"And *I* told *you* to cancel your plans, you're spending the night with *me*!"

"Just because we fucked once or twice, doesn't mean you own me!" He pushed past her and retrieved his suit jacket.

"Pop as many cherries as you like," she answered, "it'll keep you in practice for our next late-night tryst."

"Don't get your hopes up," he scoffed as he snapped the clasp of his watch closed.

Natalia rose from the sofa and moved close to him. They stood face to face, the atmosphere electric between them, and Xavier couldn't hide his body's involuntary reaction to her advances.

"Oh, come on, Xavier, you know you want this," she said, licking her lips as she slid her hands down the length of his torso. Xavier grabbed them before they reached their destination.

"Seriously, Natalia, after you've ridden the roller coaster a few times, the thrill is gone."

Natalia jerked her hands from his; her eyes narrowed. *"How dare you!"* Xavier laughed. A knock at the door interrupted them.

"Come in!" Xavier called.

Richard opened the door and entered, followed by Xavier's current 'dinner date'. "Oh, hello Ms. Devon… ready to go, X?

Xavier gathered his belongings and handed the bags to Richard. "I'll meet you in the car."

"Okay," Richard said, "goodnight Ms. Devon."

The assistant left with the young lady in tow. Xavier picked up his guitar case and stepped toward the door. He stopped and turned toward the woman.

"Try not to be angry, Nat, it doesn't look good on you. You're a gorgeous woman, and you're a hell of a lay, but I can't commit to you. We both knew that from the start. We've had some fun, some laughs… some unforgettable nights together, don't try to make this into something it's not." He opened the door, then paused. "Oh, one more thing…" He set the instrument down and walked toward her. She cowered as he pulled her close and gave her a final kiss, his tongue penetrating her lips and delving deep, taking her breath away. She pushed against him until he released his grasp; he went back to the door. "…don't ever try to control me again, Natalia." He picked up the guitar case. *"Ever!"*

She jumped as Xavier slammed the door, leaving her alone. Natalia composed herself, then glanced in the mirror to check her appearance before leaving the dressing room. She walked toward the exit that led to the parking lot where Xavier's limo was waiting. The guard opened the door and she stepped through, stopping when she saw them. Xavier was taking selfies with fans and signing autographs while Richard waited with Xavier's latest one-night stand.

Natalia inwardly seethed as she watched them. She knew it was because of her that Xavier was a great lover. It was because of her guidance, her patience. She was the one who taught him how to treat a woman; how to touch her, kiss her, talk to her. It was she, Natalia Devon, who taught him how to make love to a woman, to pleasure her to the point that she would do anything he asked of her. She was the one who made him into the lover he was, and he had left her behind, cast aside like a soiled garment.

Her eyes were glued to Xavier as he touched the young woman's face, then leaned in to kiss her. They sat down in the limo and Natalia watched as the car pulled away and drove in the direction of Xavier's hotel.

"You will live to regret this day, Xavier Kaine."

## Chapter 24

Xavier stepped out from the bedroom just as Richard entered the suite. "Richard, thank God you're here!"

"I just got your message, what's wrong?"

"I can't sleep."

"Are you sick?"

"No."

"Is there something on your mind, anything you want to talk about?"

"No."

"Then what's the problem?"

"I can't sleep, that's my problem!!" Richard stood silent as Xavier paced back and forth. "I'm sorry, I don't mean to yell. I'm just so tired." He stopped and looked at Richard. "You wouldn't happen to have any of those pills, would you?"

Richard hesitated, then pulled the small box from the pocket of his suit jacket. Xavier smiled when he saw it. "Could I?" he asked. Richard opened the box and took out a single pill, placing it in Xavier's hand.

"I need more."

"X, you're only supposed to take one."

"One doesn't work, I need more."

Richard sighed; against his better judgement, he dumped another pill into Xavier's palm. The man curled the fingers of his hand toward himself to indicate he wanted more.

*"Three?!"*

"I can't sleep, Richard!"

"No, I've given you too much already," he said, waving him off as he walked away.

Xavier looked at the white pills. He walked over to Richard and held out his hand. "Here," he said.

Richard opened his hand and Xavier dropped the pills into it. "I thought you needed them."

"There's no sense in taking them, they won't help."

"They make you drowsy, don't they?"

"Yeah, but I need to *sleep*. I can't go out on that stage half-awake, I can't play like that. I'd be slurring my words and stumbling around… what if I fell off the stage?"

"Two pills won't help you fall asleep?"

"No."

"But three would?" Xavier stared at him. Richard wavered for a minute, but finally shook his head. "I can't, X, I'm sorry. It's too many."

"Never mind," Xavier said as he moved to the sofa and switched on the TV.

"It's not safe, you could overdose," Richard explained as his boss sat silent, "Please don't be angry with me."

"Just go, Richard."

Xavier flipped from channel to channel until Richard left, then switched the set off. The room was quiet... *excruciatingly* quiet. When he was onstage with all the lights and the crowd and the music swirling around him, he was in his element. What he came back to afterward—the perfectly-kept, perfectly-decorated, extremely expensive hotel suites—was becoming his own personal hell. Richard would make sure he got back to the hotel safely and that he had everything he needed, then he would leave Xavier alone until the next morning when it was time to catch a flight to the next city. It didn't matter what the name on the front of the building was, they were all the same. Every hotel was the same, every face was the same, every city was the same... night after night after night.

Xavier stood from the sofa and moved to the bar where he poured a couple fingers of vodka over a few cubes of ice and drank half in the first gulp. The second swallow emptied the glass and he promptly refilled it. He turned as he raised the glass to his lips but stopped when his eyes caught sight of something on the opposite side of the room. On closer inspection, he found it to be the silver pill box that Richard had held onto so tightly. Xavier smiled to himself as he picked it up and headed for the bedroom.

## Chapter 25

Richard opened the bedroom door and popped his head in. "Hey X, we're ordering dinner. You want steak?"

"Pecan pie," a deep, solemn voice replied through the darkness.

"What?"

"Pecan pie."

"For dinner?" Richard scoffed. "They have a whole menu, X, why don't you try some baby back ribs or…"

"Pecan pie!"

"Fine, I'll see if they have pecan pie. Do you want the ribs, too?"

"I JUST WANT PECAN PIE!!" Xavier snarled, hurling the TV remote across the bedroom. It hit the mirror like a spear, sending shards of glass onto the dresser and carpet below. Richard flinched and turned to avoid the jagged pieces that flew in his direction. He looked in shock at his boss; Xavier stared at the floor, red-faced and haggard looking. Neither of them spoke.

Through moonlit shadows, Richard could see the man's angry expression; could hear his heavy breaths. He was afraid to move. Xavier stood at least half a foot taller than him and outweighed him by several pounds of pure muscle mass. He could easily take Richard down.

The ruckus attracted the attention of the others in the suite, and Miles opened the bedroom door, illuminating Richard's half of the room. "Everything okay in here?"

"X was just telling me what he wants for dinner."

"I see, and what have we decided on?"

There was a long pause as Miles waited.

"I want pecan pie."

"Pecan pie?" Xavier nodded slowly without looking up. "Well, I think we can make that happen," Miles said.

"But it's not on the menu."

The big man clenched his fists at his side and emitted a low, throaty growl. Miles shot a stiff glare at the assistant.

*"Make it happen,"* he instructed slowly, his voice calm yet demanding. He gave a quick nod toward the door and Richard hurried out. Miles took a visual assessment of the bedroom—the broken mirror, the pieces of glass scattered about, the television remote lying amongst them. "You want coffee with your pie?"

Xavier's eyes stay focused on the floor. "Milk."

"I'll order some. You might want to put some shoes on, don't want to cut yourself on all this glass." Miles stepped out and closed the door behind him.

Xavier stood alone in the darkness. His heart and his head were both pounding, their back-and-forth cadence making him feel dizzy and sick to his stomach. He started back to the bed, but only got a few steps before he felt a searing jab on the bottom of his bare foot.

"FUCK!" He hobbled the remaining distance and sat on the edge of the bed to examine the cut. A small shard of glass protruded from just below the space between his first two toes. He winced as he pulled the fragment out, then licked his thumb and cleaned the blood from his foot. He inspected the glass for a second before flicking it toward the dresser. It made a hard *click* as it bounced off the piece of furniture.

Xavier looked toward the mirror. In the dim light, he could see his reflection, distorted by the web of cracks. He could hear the voices — *'Xavier Kaine!'… 'Over here!'… 'This way!'… 'We love you, Xavier!'*. He could hear them everywhere, constantly talking, needing, wanting… they never stopped. A bolt of pain pierced through his temple. He closed his eyes and curled up in a fetal position.

*'Xavier!'*
*'I want your autograph!'*
*'Look this way, Xavier!'*

He grabbed a pillow and held it tight around his head.

*'I'm your biggest fan!'*
*'Xavier Kaine!'*

"Shut up!"

*'Xavier!'*
*'XAVIER KAINE!!!'*

"SHUT UP! SHUT UP! FOR CHRIST'S SAKE, SHUT UP!!!"

Richard returned to the hotel suite, slightly out of breath, beads of sweat across his forehead. He walked over to the table where the others were enjoying their dinner and set a cake box down beside Miles' plate. Miles looked up at him.

"Pecan pie."

Miles grinned. "Well done." Richard pulled a chair up to the table and joined the meal as Miles called room service and ordered the milk Xavier had requested.

## Chapter 26

*"Eugene!"*

The man stirred in his sleep.

*"Eugene!"*

The voice jolted him awake, and he sat up fast, like a bullet shot from a gun. A searing ache moved through his skull and he jumped from the bed, making a beeline to the bathroom. His knees hit hard against the tile as he bent over the porcelain, his stomach lurching and heaving. A few minutes later he sat sweaty and crumpled, wiping his mouth with one of the plush hotel towels.

It took him a few minutes to remember where he was, not that he cared much. Random memories of the night before bounced around in his mind—talking with Richard, loud voices… and there was something about pie.

Xavier spread the towel out and draped it over his head and face as he sat alone in the coolness of the darken bathroom. His abdominal muscles cramped every now and then and he massaged them with his hands to keep whatever was left in his stomach where it was.

Richard tapped on the bedroom door. "X?" He peeked in, the sun brightening the interior enough for him to see the empty bed. "X, you in here?"

He stepped in and looked around for signs of life. When he reached the bathroom doorway, he could make out a large shadow on the floor by the toilet. "X?" The assistant flipped the light switch to see better.

"Turn that goddamn light off!" A swift move of Richard's hand sent the room into half-light once more.

"Are you okay?" Xavier lifted the front of the towel and peered up at him. "Jesus, X, you look like shit!"

"Thank you for that astute observation, Richard," he answered, his voice thick with sarcasm. He lowered the edge of the towel.

"Your feet are bloody."

Xavier pulled his legs toward him and examined the soles of both feet. Fresh bright red blood dripped from several spots and mixed with the darker crusted blood from prior cuts. Tiny slivers of glass glimmered in the faint daylight from the adjacent room.

"What the hell..." He picked the pieces from his skin and dropped them one by one into the toilet bowl. "What happened last night?"

"You broke the mirror."

*"What?"*

"You threw the remote and broke the mirror. There's glass all over the carpet."

"That explains the cuts," Xavier concluded, "but why would I throw the remote?" He paused as he pulled the towel from his head. "And why do I keep thinking about pie?"

"You threw the remote because you were mad."

"About what?"

"Pie."

Xavier stopped messing with his injured feet and looked at his assistant. "You're not making any sense, Richard."

"You were mad about the pie."

*"What pie?!"*

"The pecan pie," Richard explained, "You wanted pecan pie for dinner, and it wasn't on the menu." Xavier rested his cheekbone on his thumb and rubbed his forehead with the other four fingers as he searched his brain for the specific memory. "You kinda threw a fit and insisted on having pecan pie, so I went out and found some for you. It's on the tray by the door."

Xavier was quiet for a moment. "Did I hurt anyone?"

"Just your feet," he answered with a nod.

"I'm sorry, Richard."

"It's okay, X, we all get grouchy when we're tired. Come on, let's get you cleaned up."

Richard helped Xavier up from the tile floor and into the shower. He cleaned up the blood and as much of the glass as he could, then located a member of the housekeeping staff to do a quick vacuuming.

## Chapter 27

Xavier stood under the showerhead hoping the warmth of the flowing water would help bring him out of the haze he was currently experiencing. Try as he might, he couldn't remember the events that Richard had recounted to him. He couldn't deny their truth, though, he had the cuts on his feet to prove it.

He stepped from the shower, his sore feet stinging, and patted himself dry before making use of one of the complimentary robes the hotel provided for its guests. At the sink, he brushed his teeth—twice—and swished some Scope around the inside of his mouth, gargling to remove any last traces of what his stomach had rejected. He spit the minty green liquid in the sink and rinsed it down the drain just as Richard knocked on the door.

"Come in," he called as he pulled a comb through his wet hair.

"I got some ointment and Band-Aids for your feet."

"They're okay, Richard, really."

"We have to make sure they don't get infected, now sit."

Xavier limped over and sat on the side of the tub. Richard lowered the lid of the toilet and sat down, placing his supplies on top of the tank. He pulled the halves of the Band-Aid wrappers apart and opened the ointment.

"Gimme your foot."

"This really isn't necessary."

"Let me see your foot," Richard repeated. The man sighed and did as requested. After both feet were bandaged, Richard held out a pair of slippers emblazoned with the hotel's monogram. "I cleaned up the glass, but just in case…" Xavier put them on and the two men walked out to the bedroom. "You get dressed and I'll call Miles, then we can get some breakfast." He opened the bedroom door.

"Hey Richard?"

"Yeah?"

"Thanks… you know, for the pie and…"

"Anytime, X." He smiled and left the room.

Xavier glanced at the bureau. There was the pie, just where Richard said it was. A glass of milk, no doubt warm from sitting out all night, stood on the tray beside it. He drew closer and gave it a once-over. The thought of eating anything turned him off because of the episode with his stomach earlier, but the longer he looked at it, the more he wanted it.

He reached out and plucked a pecan from the top of the slice, then laid it on his tongue and rolled it around before crunching down on it. As Xavier chewed, a memory stirred in his subconscious… *It was a cool, crisp autumn morning at the farm. A young boy was sitting at the kitchen table, a basket of freshly-harvested pecan nuts on the floor beside him. He was cracking open the shells and depositing their contents into a large bowl…*

Xavier lifted the plate and fork from the tray and took a small taste. Brown sugar, honey, butter—his mother used to make pecan pies like this. They would eat it warm, topped with homemade vanilla ice cream. Every now and then, she would add a little bourbon whiskey to the recipe. His father never did figure out what her 'secret ingredient' was.

Is that why he had wanted pecan pie so badly, because it reminded him of his mother? He sat on the corner of the bed, his feet throbbing in the hotel slippers, and finished the slice of pie, then returned the plate to the tray.

When he turned to get dressed, he caught sight of himself in the shattered dresser mirror and his splintered image shocked him. He stopped, then moved closer, pausing every couple of steps, observing how the image changed. When he was close enough, he reached out and touched the thick glass.

He ran his index finger along the uneven edges of the cracks and watched as drops of blood trickled down the smooth surface until they reached the next break and began to pool. The puddle grew wider as more of the life force oozed from the deepening cut on his finger. It soon overflowed, sending several new streams down the unbroken sections of the mirror simultaneously.

Xavier stepped back from the dresser and watched as his blood mingled with his fragmented reflection. His hands started to shake as a paralyzing fear took hold of him; his heart beat faster and faster until he could hardly breathe; his entire body was wet with perspiration. He grabbed at the robe, causing smears of red from his bleeding hand. All at once, he felt closer to death than he ever had before.

"Richard," he called out, but there was no answer. "Richard! Richard!" Xavier felt his knees buckling and he fell back onto the carpet. Tears soaked his cheeks as he began to hyperventilate, and he crab-crawled backward as far as he could away from the dresser.

"RICHARD!!!" he screamed at the top of his lungs, "RICHARD!!! RICHARD, HELP ME!!! RICHARD!!!"

## Chapter 28

"RICHAAAAARRRRDDD!!!!"

Miles and Richard stopped in the hallway just outside the hotel suite, each with a curious expression.

"Did you just hear something," Miles asked, "like someone yelling?

"I think so, must be a party in one of the other suites."

Miles shrugged and opened the door to the hotel room.

"RICHARD!!! RICHARD, I CAN'T BREATHE!!! SOMEONE PLEASE HELP ME!!!!"

The men bolted to the bedroom where they found Xavier curled up on the floor against the bureau. The white terrycloth robe he was wearing, as well as the carpet around him were smeared with blood.

"RICHARD, WHERE ARE YOU?! I NEED YOU!!!" he screamed between hysterical sobs.

The assistant dropped down beside him. "I'm here, X! I'm right here!"

"RICHARD!!"

"I'm here! I'm here!" He grabbed the large lapels of the robe and pulled Xavier toward him. "I'm here, X! I'm right in front of you!" Xavier screamed again; his eyes wide with fear.

"He's hallucinating!" Miles exclaimed.

Richard pulled Xavier closer. "Look at me, X! LOOK AT ME!!! *LOOK AT ME, XAVIER!!*" He gave the confused man a forceful shake and Xavier's mind snapped back into reality, his eyes focusing on the assistant's face.

"Richard?" he managed through sobs and quick breaths.

"I'm here, X," he confirmed, "just breathe…" Richard waited and watched, but the pace of Xavier's respirations remained rapid. "BREATHE WITH ME, X! COME ON, BREATHE WITH ME!!" Richard took in deep breaths and blew them out slowly. Xavier grasped hold of Richard's hands as they held tight to the robe and did his best to imitate his friend's breathing…

Breathe in… breathe out… breathe in… breathe out… breathe in… breath out…

Xavier's heart rate slowed to normal…

Breathe in… breathe out… breathe in… breathe out…
breathe in… breath out…

Xavier's tense muscles eased…

"That's it, nice and easy," Richard instructed, "Just keep
breathing, X. We're all here, everything's gonna be all right…
You're gonna be all right."

Xavier looked up at him, tears filling his frightened eyes.
The assistant took his boss in his arms and pulled him close. Xavier
held tight to Richard, letting go of his fear through a storm of tears.

"We should call 911."

"Doctor's on his way," Miles told him, "Where's the blood
coming from?"

Richard did a fast check. "Looks like he sliced his finger
open, but I don't know what he cut it on…"

"I do." Richard looked up at Miles who pointed at the
dresser. Richard turned to see the mirror, Xavier's blood seeping
through the cracked maze.

"My god…"

There was a knock at the door of the suite and Miles went
to answer it. Richard lowered Xavier back down to the floor and
started to stand, but Xavier latched onto his hands again, a look of
pure terror on his face.

"Don't worry, I won't leave you."

Miles returned with the doctor and the three of them moved
Xavier back to the bed. Richard stood with Miles as the doctor
repaired the injured finger. They spoke in hushed tones while the
doctor finished his examination.

"What happened here, Richard?"

"I don't know." Miles looked at him, unsatisfied with the
man's answer. "I really don't, Miles! He was in the bathroom when
I got here. He took a shower and he was starting to get dressed
when I left. Fifteen minutes later, we came back and he was
screaming."

The doctor approached them and sighed. "He had a panic
attack," he stated bluntly.

"A panic attack?" The doctor nodded. "But he was fine
when I left him."

"What would cause him to have a panic attack?" Miles asked.

"There's really no way to tell what triggered it, although there are several things that can make a person more susceptible to panic attacks, like high anxiety, stress, traumatic events, drug and alcohol use…"

"Could he have another one of these attacks?" Richard asked.

"There's always a possibility. No one can really predict when they'll occur; we can only hope this was a one-time thing. No guarantees, though." Richard and Miles glanced at each other.

Miles sighed. "So, what now?"

"I put five stitches in his finger, should take about a week to heal, and I gave him a sedative. He'll sleep for several hours, but he should make a full recovery."

"You gave him a sedative?" Miles asked, clearly annoyed.

"Yes," the doctor answered, "The man is exhausted, Mr. Sharpe, what he needs now is plenty of rest. See that he gets it."

Miles agreed, and the doctor showed himself out. They stood observing Xavier.

"I guess we'll have to cancel the show."

"We're not cancelling."

"What are you talking about, we *have* to cancel."

"We are *not* cancelling the show."

"Miles…"

"Xavier Kaine will be on that stage tonight."

"How's he gonna play with five stitches in his finger?"

"He'll manage."

"But he's *sedated*, Miles! The doctor said he'd be asleep for hours!"

Miles stared at the slumbering musician. He glanced at Richard with half a smile, then looked back to Xavier.

"What are you gonna do?" Richard asked him, but the man just walked away. "Miles?... Miles!"

Richard had a bad feeling in the pit of his stomach. Miles was up to something, that much he knew, but what? He walked over and sat on the bed beside Xavier. He smoothed the hair at the sleeping man's temple and watched him as he dozed peacefully.

"I won't let him hurt you," he whispered. He lifted Xavier's injured hand up to his lips and kissed it gently. "I promise."

Chapter 29

Xavier heard a knock on his hotel room door and jerked it open. "Hello, Richard!" He turned and hurried into the bedroom.

"Hello, X," Richard answered, watching as Xavier zipped around the suite, "I came to help you get ready…"

"For the show? No need, I'm ready."

"You are?"

"Of course, I am! Let's go!" Xavier grabbed his guitar case and left the suite. Richard followed him out into the hallway, doing his best to match the man's frantic pace.

"Are you feelin' all right, Boss?"

"I feel *fantastic!*" The two men boarded the elevator and traveled down to the hotel lobby. Xavier rushed outside to the limo, then looked back toward the door. "Come on, Richard!" The two men climbed into the car and the driver sped off.

They arrived at the back lot of the arena, and Xavier had one foot out the door before the car came to a complete stop; he dashed over to greet his fans. Richard stepped out with Xavier's guitar and closed the door. He waited a few seconds and observed the man before joining him at the fence.

"You forgot this," Richard said as he held up the case.

"Thanks! Hey, have you all met my assistant, Richard?" Xavier wrapped his arm tight around Richard's shoulders. "This guy can do *anything*!" A spattering of hellos came from the crowd; Richard nodded, embarrassed by the attention. "You'd better be ready for tonight, cause this show is gonna be *HOT!*" The fans responded with mass hysteria, heightening Xavier's adrenaline level. "Come on, Richard, let's heat this place up!"

Xavier led his assistant by the shoulders toward the backstage entrance. They met Miles just inside the door.

"Miles, my man!"

"Hello, Xavier!" They shook hands, and Xavier headed to his dressing room. "Hello, Richard!" Miles smiled broadly at him, then went back to his work.

Richard stood alone in the entryway. Something wasn't right with Xavier, he could feel it, and he knew Miles had something to do with it. He proceeded down the lengthy corridor. When he reached the dressing room, he could hear female voices and laughter coming from the opposite side of the door; he knocked.

"X?"

"Richard, come in!" The assistant opened the door to find his boss flanked by two young ladies. "We've been waiting for you. I want you to meet my two biggest fans!" Xavier introduced them, and Richard listened as the fans praised Xavier.

"It's time to go, X," Richard told him.

"Oh, come on, Richard, we can partake in the company of these lovely ladies for a little while longer, can't we?"

"We're due on stage for the sound check, sorry girls."

"Enjoy the show, you two!" Xavier said as he and Richard started to leave; he paused. "I was just wondering, would the two of you like to have dinner with me after the show?" They gladly accepted, and the star blew them each a kiss. "Take care of the details for me, Richard."

"Sure X, no problem," he answered as Xavier disappeared in the tangle of backstage passageways. Richard made the necessary arrangements with the 'dinner dates', then went to join Miles in the sound booth.

## Chapter 30

"I'm doing the best I can, Mr. Kaine!"

"Well your best isn't worth a *fuck*! Leave it, I'll do it myself!"

Richard entered the dressing room. Xavier stood in front of the mirror adjusting his clothes while a teary-eyed wardrobe woman waited nearby.

"Is there a problem in here?"

Xavier turned to him. "Look at this, Richard!" Xavier said, pulling at his shirt.

"What's wrong with it?"

"It looks like shit! I can't wear this onstage!"

"Calm down, X, we can get you a different shirt." Richard moved closer to the frightened woman. "I'm sorry, I'm sure he didn't mean to upset you. It's not your fault. You can go, I'll take care of it," he whispered. She nodded and made a hasty retreat.

Richard chose another shirt from the wardrobe closet and gave it to Xavier. The man fumbled with the buttons until he finally gave up and slumped down in his chair in defeat. Richard laid his hand on Xavier's shoulder. The musician stood and let Richard button his shirt.

"Where's Miles?"

"Probably backstage," Richard answered, "why?"

"I need to talk to him."

"We'll see him when we go out to the stage…"

"NO!" Xavier exclaimed; Richard took a step back. "I need to see him now."

"I'll see if I can find him."

Xavier waited until Richard was gone, then fell back in the chair again. He rested his forehead on the heal of his hand. A few moments later, he felt his stomach churn and made his way to the bathroom where he stayed until Miles knocked.

"Richard said you wanted to talk to me."

"I think the medicine the doctor gave me is wearing off."

"There's only a few left…"

"Please, Miles, I can't go out there like this."

Miles took a bottle from the pocket of his suit jacket and poured a pill into Xavier's hand. "We start in about fifteen minutes, are you gonna be ready?"

"I'll be ready." Miles patted his back and left the room. Xavier gulped the pill down with some water, then squatted down and laid his sweaty cheek against the cool porcelain of the sink basin. He closed his eyes and waited…

Chapter 31

Miles returned from the dressing room and met up with Richard in the wings.

"Where's X?"

"He'll be here."

"He's usually out here by now..."

"Relax, Richard, he'll be here." Miles moved the edge of the curtain and eyeballed the crowd; a second later, the house lights went dark.

"Miles, *where is he*?" Richard asked.

Before Miles could answer, a lightning-fast guitar riff was heard through the massive speakers that surrounded the stage. Richard swung around to see Xavier approaching from behind.

Xavier grinned wide, an intense determination on his face, his fingers flying over the strings of the guitar as the crowd went wild. He drew close, his eyes riveted on Richard's. He played faster and faster and moved closer and closer until they were face to face; so close that he feel the vibrations of Xavier's guitar strings; so close, Richard could see his face in the pupils of Xavier's eyes. Then, in a split second, he was onstage, catering to the legions of fans that filled the arena.

For several long moments, Richard couldn't move, every inch of his body held captive by the mystique of Xavier Kaine. Day by day, it was getting more difficult for Richard to hide his feelings. Was it possible that Xavier had figured out his secret? His actions over the last few minutes would indicate he had, but how could Richard be sure?

Xavier's voice surged through the arena and woke Richard from his thoughts. Xavier played wicked and wild, giving the people all he had to satisfy their unquenchable thirst for him. He fed on their enthusiasm as the show reached a fever pitch.

Richard got a feeling while watching Xavier perform, but it was different than the one he had just minutes before. This was a bad feeling deep in his gut that he'd had since he picked Xavier up from the hotel.

Earlier, the doctor had told them the sedative would make Xavier sleep for several hours, yet there he was on the stage, performing with more energy than Richard had ever seen. Then there was the episode in the dressing room with the woman from the wardrobe department… it was all so bizarre. The man on that stage wasn't the Xavier Kaine he knew.

Miles came up beside Richard, crossed his arms and stood watching; he wore a smug expression. "Told you he'd be ready," he said without moving his gaze.

Richard felt his face warm with anger. "What did you give him?"

"I didn't give him anything."

"The mood swings, the excess energy, the extreme highs and lows… I know he's on something, Miles, now what is it?"

"I gave him a Dexedrine."

"You gave him uppers?"

"It's no big deal, Richard, once this one wears off, he'll sleep like a baby."

*"This one??"*

"Yes, this one."

"How long has he been taking it?"

"I gave him one earlier this afternoon, then another in the dressing room before the show."

Richard's anger grew, along with his concern for Xavier. "Does he know?"

"Of course not, he thinks the doctor prescribed it for him."

"No more."

"I beg your pardon?"

"I said, *no more*."

A moment of silence fell between them.

"I do believe you've forgotten your place, Richard," Miles stated, "It's my job to make the decisions. It's your job…"

"To keep Xavier happy."

"Correct, and you've done an excellent job."

"I'm not so sure."

Miles glanced out at the stage. "He looks happy to me," he commented with a laugh, "You just keep him that way, and we won't have any problems, okay, Richard?" He walked away, his footsteps fast, but Richard gave chase and caught him by the arm.

"You're not going to give him any more of that shit, Miles, do you hear me?! *No more!!*"

"Careful boy…"

"I mean it, Miles! I've worked for you long enough to know your little tricks, and you're not fooling anyone! I'll tell X about all of it – the extortion, the lies, the manipulation, the drugs – *everything!*"

Miles smiled; he sighed and shook his head. All at once, he clamped his hand around Richard's throat and slammed him against a nearby wall.

"*You are not going to tell anyone anything!!* I have worked too hard for too long to let a lousy little prick like you get in my way!"

Richard pulled at Miles' hand as he struggled to breath. Miles moved his face in until his nose was pressing against Richard's cheek. He tightened his grip; Richard felt his throat constrict. Miles was silent for a few moments, as the man fought desperately to breath, then spoke slowly into his ear.

"Don't mess with me, Richard, because I will *fucking destroy you!*" With a flick of his wrist, Miles threw Richard aside like a rag doll and calmly strolled away. Richard lay in a heap in the concrete floor, coughing and gasping for air. Once he had regained his composure, he stood and stepped to the wings of the stage; he looked out at Xavier.

"You may destroy me, Miles, but I won't let you destroy him."

## Chapter 32

"Richard?" Xavier opened the bedroom door. "Richard!"

"What's the matter, Xavier?"

"I'm hungry."

"Okay, I'll order some breakfast. Do you want anything in particular?"

"It doesn't matter, just get it here!" Xavier pushed the door shut.

Richard sighed as he wrapped his robe around himself and tied the belt. He yawned as he picked up the room service menu from the desk and took it to the sofa. He read through it, choosing items for both Xavier and he, then dialed the phone.

"Hello?... Yes, I'd like to order breakfast for ... What?... Seven?" Richard glanced at his watch. "Shit... Listen, I'm calling from Mr. Kaine's suite... Yes, Xavier Kaine, he has to catch a plane in a couple of hours, and he was hoping to have breakfast before he leaves... I understand you don't open for another hour, but couldn't you make an exception just this once?" Richard waited on hold while the young lady on the other end of the line went to find her supervisor.

Since the incident with Miles, Richard had made it a point to share a suite with Xavier, so he could keep an eye on him and protect him as much as possible, but no matter how close he stayed, Miles was still able to isolate Xavier enough to control him. He decided not to confront Miles again. Doing so would put his job in jeopardy, and he didn't want to risk leaving Xavier alone with no one except Miles to depend on. For now, he would have to stay as close as he could and hold his tongue.

The kitchen supervisor came on the line and took the food order; Richard hung up the phone. He lay back on the sofa and closed his eyes. After a short while, he felt a hand on his shoulder. He opened his eyes and blinked. Xavier was sitting on the coffee table beside him; he was showered and dressed. He waited for Richard to get his bearings.

"Good morning," he said with a smile.

"Good morning."

"They brought breakfast, if you're hungry." Xavier walked around the sofa to the table. Richard sat up and looked over at the food. He had slept through the knock from room service.

"What time is it?" he asked as he joined his friend at the table.

"Close to seven." Xavier piled some scrambled eggs on a plate, then added bacon, sausage and potatoes. He set the plate in front of Richard.

"That's a lot of food, X."

"Your body needs more than coffee, Richard. Besides, I'm enjoying the company."

Richard smiled. "Me, too."

They sat eating and talking for almost an hour about anything that entered their minds. There were moments when they giggled like schoolgirls and moments when Xavier shared some of his most intimate thoughts and feelings, but the ones Richard most enjoyed were the moments in between, when the conversation lulled, and it was silent; when it was just the two of them alone together…

The ringing of Richard's cell phone interrupted their solitude. He answered it, spoke few words and ended the call. Immediately he started cleaning up.

"Was it Miles?" Xavier asked.

"Yes, he's on his way up."

"You go get dressed, I'll take care of this."

"He'll be here in a few minutes!"

Xavier took hold of Richard's hands; their eyes met. "I'll take care of him, too, now go."

Richard laughed and sprinted into the bedroom. Xavier straightened up some and gathered their suitcases, placing them neatly by the door. Richard emerged from the bedroom just as Miles' keycard clicked in the door lock; Miles opened the door.

"Ready?"

Xavier grinned at him. "Aren't we always?"

Miles' suspicious eyes moved back and forth between them. "Let's go!" he commanded. Xavier glanced at Richard; he smiled and winked, then followed Miles down the hallway. A bellman loaded their bags on a trolley while Richard waited. He felt the butterflies in his stomach flutter; he smiled to himself and left the suite.

Chapter 33

Xavier stood on the stage, soaked in sweat, the lights around him pulsating furiously to a beat so strong it saturated everything within earshot. The energy that drove him seemed endless; the spontaneous riffs he created were like none anyone had ever heard before. It was the best show he had ever done, but in his gut, he knew something was off. He couldn't put his finger on it, but he could feel the show dragging, and he played at a frenzied pace to keep it alive. When he came off the stage, he was barely able to stand.

"They want more!"

"Don't do the encore, X, you're worn out!"

"I have to, they're expecting it!" He pushed Richard away and went back out into the spotlight.

"Xavier!" Richard called out, but there was no way for him to be heard over the blaring guitar. Xavier gave them everything he had, and they responded in kind as he left the stage again. Richard wrapped a towel around the musician's neck as they headed for the dressing room.

"Something was wrong tonight."

"Wrong with what?"

"With the show, Richard, didn't you feel it?"

"You've got to be kidding, X, that was the most incredible show you've ever done."

"I'm telling you, something was off!"

They reached the dressing room and Xavier went in alone. He showered and put on fresh clothes, then stood at the sink. After wiping the condensation from the mirror, he looked at the man staring back at him. He knew he was looking at the person everyone knew as Xavier Kaine, but he felt like he was looking at a stranger.

"X!"

"In here!" He pulled his thoughts together as Richard peeked around the bathroom doorway.

"You're date's here."

"My date?" Richard gave him a look. "Oh, my date, right."

"I'll be out in the hall."

He nodded, and Richard disappeared. Xavier leaned around the door frame and saw a pretty young girl in a yellow dress standing alone in his dressing room. He left the confines of the bathroom and stood a minute, watching her.

"Hello."

She spun around. "Hello."

"What's your name?"

"Chelsea."

Xavier walked closer. "I'm Xavier," he said. They stared at each other for several seconds. No matter what he tried to say, it wouldn't come out. The words stuck like glue in his throat.

"Are you okay?" she asked.

"I just… I'm sorry, I just need a minute."

The dressing room door opened, and Xavier quickly stepped out into the hallway. He stood, eyes closed, heart racing, with his back to the door. Richard, who had been standing like a sentry guarding the entrance, turned in surprise.

"What are you doing out here?"

"I can't do this," Xavier told him.

"What? Why? What did she do?"

"She didn't do anything."

"That damn little tease!"

"She's not a tease…"

"She *is* a virgin, isn't she? Dammit, X, she told me she was, I swear!"

"Richard, stop! She didn't do anything because I didn't *ask* her to do anything."

The man looked at his boss, half concerned and half astonished. "Are you feeling all right?"

"I'm fine, I just can't do this anymore."

"Should I call a doctor?" his assistant joked.

Xavier shot him a look and went back inside the dressing room. The young woman stood from her chair, her delicate mouth forming a tentative smile as she waited for him to make the next move. Xavier smiled at her.

"Hi."

"Hi," she echoed.

"What's your name again?"

"Chelsea."

"Chelsea, right," he said as he picked up a marker and autographed a picture for her. "Listen, Chelsea, I appreciate your support and I'm really glad you enjoyed the show…"

"I LOVED IT! I have all your CD's and I have a HUGE scrapbook and it's full of all kinds of pictures of you and articles about you and your music and I'm a lifetime member of your fan club and I wore this dress because I just knew you'd like it, you do like it, don't you? OH MY GOD, I CAN'T BELIEVE I'M IN YOUR DRESSING ROOM!!!!" Her words bursting out like sparks from a firework.

"Wow… and you said all of that in one breath!" He looked at her in amazement. "Maybe you should sit down for a minute."

"Oh no, I'm fine. I've got *lots* of energy!"

He laughed. "I can see that."

"Are we going?"

"Going?"

"To dinner. That guy… um, what's his name?"

"Richard?"

"That's him, he said you noticed me during the show and wanted to know if I'd be your date."

"Oh yeah, I did," he answered, "but I really don't think I'll be able to go out to dinner with you tonight."

Chelsea's expression changed to one of genuine concern. "Why, are you sick?"

"No, I'm fine, it's just that with all the traveling and interviews and the show… truth is, I'm just exhausted. It's already close to midnight and I have an early flight tomorrow. I'm just gonna go back to the hotel and order room service…"

"I don't mind room service, I'll come with you…"

"I don't think that's a good idea, Chelsea."

"It's the dress, isn't it? You don't like it…"

"No, I do like it, it's a beautiful dress. I just don't think you should come back to my hotel room," Xavier explained as he led her to the door.

"It's me then." She turned to face him, her eyes brimming with tears. "It's me you don't like."

"Chelsea, you're a beautiful young lady, but I can't go out with you tonight."

"Please Xavier!"

"I'm sorry, but I just can't." He opened the door. "Richard, will you please make sure Chelsea gets home safely?"

"Sure thing, X."

Chelsea's bottom lip quivered as Xavier kissed her lightly on the cheek, closed the dressing room door and fastened the bolt.

A peculiar feeling came over him as he leaned against the door. His pulse quickened, causing the veins in his head to hammer. With the heels of his hands, he pressed with all his might against his temples until the pain subsided.

His hand found the switch and with a slight push, he plunged the room into darkness, then made his way to the small sofa and curled up on its soft cushions. A blast of air cooled his sweaty head as the air conditioner kicked on and he put a throw pillow over his face to block the draft. A few minutes later he was sleeping soundly.

## Chapter 34

A light knocking woke him.

"Who is it?"

"It's Richard." Xavier rubbed the sleep from his eyes as he opened the door for his assistant. "Are you all right?" Richard asked.

Xavier sighed. "I'm fine."

"Really? I mean, a little while ago you were…"

"I'm just tired of it, Richard."

"Tired of what?"

"Everything! The cameras, the reporters, people following me around all hours of the day and night tracking everything I say and do trying to get the next big headline… I'm just sick and tired of this whole damn mess!"

"But this is what you've worked for, this is what you've wanted your entire life!"

"What I *wanted* was for my music to be recognized. What I *wanted* was to be looked up to and respected as an artist, not to be hunted down in the streets like a stray dog with a new bitch to hump every week! Those people don't care what I do, they only care *who* I do! This pathetic existence of a life has got to end!"

"Wait, you're not thinkin' of…"

"Jesus, Richard, get a grip! I'm not gonna jump off a bridge, I just want to enjoy my life like everyone else!"

"But you're not like everyone else—"

"Please don't…"

"—you're special." Xavier uttered a deep growl. "C'mon Boss, let's go have a drink and get laid!"

He looked up at Richard's eager expression. "Get out, Richard."

"What'd I say?"

"GET OUT RICHARD!"

He stood and moved toward the assistant, his face red, a flash of anger in his eyes. Richard jumped and stumbled backward, groping for the door. He managed to slip through the opening just before Kaine's strong arm slammed it shut.

Xavier stood for a short while, listening as the voices of various workers mixed with the pounding and clanging of equipment as it was moved to the trucks outside. Every now and then, he would wince when screams from female fans lucky enough to win backstage passes would pierce the thick wooden door and stab his eardrums. They passed, and it was calm, but it didn't last long. The sudden screams jabbed at him again, followed by a hard knock on the door that made him jump.

"Mr. Kaine?" the security guard called out before knocking a second time, "Mr. Kaine?"

Xavier slowly turned the latch on the deadbolt and waited until the voices gave up and moved on. He could feel his heart throbbing against his breastbone; sweat dripped down his brow; his eyes darted about the dressing room; he closed them. Xavier tried to breath normally, but it was no use.

He reached to wipe the perspiration from his face and noticed that his hands—no, his *entire body* was shaking. His stomach began to cramp, and he grabbed his midsection and stumbled to the sofa to sit down until the pain passed.

*"What the hell is wrong with me?!"*

He looked at the coffee table and saw all his usual vices had been delivered for him—unopened bottles of Absolut and Jack Daniels sat on a tray alongside an unmarked packet containing various 'recreational' narcotics. He stared at the items, trying to remember why he needed them.

"Mr. Kaine?" a man's voice called as he knocked.

"Go away!"

"Mr. Kaine, your car is here."

"I said GO AWAY!!" As he stood, he grabbed the neck of the Jack Daniels bottle and slung it toward the offending voice. It crashed hard, scattering bottle fragments and sending thick caramel-colored liquid streaming down his side of the door.

"What am I doing here?" he asked aloud. Xavier dropped to the sofa. He could feel his blood surging through his arteries. It made his face hot and his head like a bomb about to explode, and he grasped his skull as if trying to stop the explosion from happening. Xavier sat back against the cushions and waited for the pressure in his head to ease enough that he could open his eyes, then blinked several times until he could finally focus on the object in front of him—his guitar. Tears flowed down his cheeks. The music. That's why he was here, for the music. How had he forgotten?

He wiped his face on his shirt sleeve as he stood and retrieved the guitar from its case. He held it close and pulled a calloused thumb across the strings. A moment later, he stood motionless, looking at the image in the large mirror on the wall opposite him. A smile began to form across his face as if he had seen a long-lost friend.

"Well… I'll be damned…"

Chapter 35

Richard walked quickly through the backstage areas of the arena and found Miles in a small office finishing up some paperwork, a secretary waiting close by.

"Miles…"

"Yeah?"

"We need to talk."

"I'm busy, Richard." He signed his name to some forms and handed them to the secretary; she hurried off.

"It's important…"

"I said I'm busy!" Miles started walking. "Shouldn't you be with X?"

"That's what I want to talk to you about."

"Go take care of X, whatever the problem is, we can talk about it later."

"I can't find him."

Miles stopped and looked at Richard. "What?"

"I can't find X."

"What the fuck are you talking about?"

"He's not here."

"Where did you see him last?"

"In his dressing room."

"Then that's where he is…"

"But he's not"

"He's probably in the bathroom."

"He's not, I checked."

"Richard, he *has* to be there!"

"And I'm telling you, *he's not*! I've searched everywhere, Miles, I can't find him!"

"Jesus, Richard, I gave you one fucking job!"

The two men headed in the direction of Xavier's dressing room. When they reached the door, Miles knocked.

"X!" He waited, but there was no answer. "Xavier!" he yelled, pounding the door with his fist, but there was only silence from the other side. Miles opened the door. A visual inventory of the room's contents—stage clothes, jewelry, personal hygiene items—told him that Xavier should still be in the building. "What was the last thing he said to you?"

"Get out."

"*Get out?*"

"Yeah, he was pissed off about something. I offered to take him out for drinks, and he threw me out."

Miles left the dressing room and weaved his way through the maze of backstage passageways; Richard followed close behind.

"What was he pissed off about?"

"How should I know?"

"Goddamn it, Richard, it's your *job* to know!" Miles stopped in one of the many hallways. "Xavier!" He paused, then shouted again. "Xavier Kaine!!" They waited, listening as the superstar's name echoed around them. "Are you sure you checked everywhere?" Miles asked as they started walking again.

"Yes."

"Did you check the limo?"

"It's still parked out back."

Miles stopped. "Did you open the door and check *inside*?" Richard stood silent and Miles rolled his eyes. "He's probably passed out in the backseat!" They exited through the stage door and walked over to the limo. Miles opened the door. "X!" He stuck his head inside the car. "Xavier!" Miles stood up straight and addressed the driver. "Where's Kaine?"

The chauffer, who had been leaning against the driver's side door smoking a cigarette, turned. "Who?"

"*Xavier Kaine*, the man you were hired to drive for, *where is he*?"

"Look, mister, I get paid to drive, not babysit."

Miles sneered at the man and the chauffer went back to his smoke. He slammed the car door and headed back into the building, pushing past arena employees and various road crew members, stopping when he reached center stage.

"XAVIER KAINE!!" he yelled at the top of his lungs. The workers all stopped and looked in Miles' direction. "Has anyone here seen Xavier Kaine in the last half-hour?"

The silence hung thick around them. Miles felt a churning in his stomach as he began to accept that Richard was right— Xavier was not in the arena. He started walking again and Richard tried hard to keep up.

"Where are you going?"

"I'm gonna check the dressing room again," he answered, "he might've come back."

Miles opened the door and stepped inside, the sweet smell of bourbon whiskey permeating his nostrils. As the door closed, he noticed the sticky dried drips that clung to the door and surrounding walls. Richard bent down and retrieved half of a broken liquor bottle from the floor. The two men looked at it but didn't speak. Miles took his phone out of his pocket.

"I tried calling him, he didn't answer."

Miles looked at him, annoyed, and dialed a number on his cell phone. Seconds later, a vibrating noise was heard coming from a far corner of the dressing room. The pair investigated and soon found the source—Xavier's cell phone.

Richard glanced around the room and noticed what looked like a credit card lying on the carpet behind a small trash can. He picked up the card and the trash can, then sat down slowly on a chair nearby.

"Miles..."

Miles turned his head toward Richard and saw him staring into the small can.

"What is it?"

Richard said nothing as he stood and walked to the dining table; Miles joined him. He carefully dumped out the can's contents. Among the normal refuse, lay an expensive leather wallet and several items that it used to hold. Miles began collecting the strewn belongings.

*"What the hell..."*

"His wallet, credit cards, driver's license... Miles, why would he leave these behind?"

"I don't know." Miles looked over the items again, then turned and scrutinized the room. "His guitar is still here."

"But he always takes it with him." Richard paused. "You don't think somebody took him, do you?" They locked eyes for several seconds as they considered the possibility. "Something is *very* wrong here, Miles. Maybe we should call the cops..."

"No, not yet," Miles said, "Stay here and call me if he comes back."

Miles began dialing as he left the room. Richard paced nervously, his imagination reeling.

Where was Xavier Kaine?

www.ingramcontent.com/pod-product-compliance
Lightning Source LLC
Chambersburg PA
CBHW070346130626
46556CB00007B/3054